The Price of Honour

A Clara Fitzgerald Mystery

Evelyn James

www.sophie-jackson.com

Contents

Chapter One	1
Chapter Two	10
Chapter Four	19
Chapter Five	27
Chapter Six	35
Chapter Seven	43
Chapter Eight	52
Chapter Nine	56
Chapter Ten	64
Chapter Eleven	71
Chapter Twelve	79
Chapter Thirteen	88
Chapter Fourteen	97
Chapter Fifteen	106
Chapter Sixteen	115
Chapter Seventeen	124
Chapter Eighteen	133
Chapter Nineteen	142

Chapter Twenty	151
Chapter Twenty-One	160
Chapter Twenty-Two	169
Chapter Twenty-Three	178
Chapter Twenty-Four	186
Chapter Twenty-Five	195
Chapter Twenty-Six	204
Chapter Twenty-Seven	213
Chapter Twenty-Eight	223
Enjoyed this Book?	237
The Clara Fitzgerald Series	238
A New Series from Evelyn James	241
About the Author	244
Copyright	246

Chapter One

The cold was making his heart pound in his chest.

Mr Nunn should have been sitting before his fire, obeying his doctor's orders, and recuperating from his recent bout of influenza, but the urgency of his task had driven him outdoors in this vile weather.

He told himself the rain didn't matter. The freezing temperature biting into his bones, did not matter. His suffering here and now, could not compare to what his son had gone through during the war. He could not even begin to imagine the horrors his boy had witnessed.

For a second, a swirl of wind battered rain into his eyes, and he had to stop and wipe away the water. In that moment he was transported to another place and time. The trenches of Belgium.

He had only served that first year, but it had been gruelling and ended up crippling him forever. The snow, the mud, the bloodshed. His heart began to pound faster as his memory slipped away to that other place where life had seemed like an endless nightmare.

Even now, he could smell the stink of rotting wood and bodies as he stood in a flooded trench, feeling the water seeping into his boots. Trench foot was on everyone's mind, but you could do nothing about it. He had caught trench foot that winter, the first stage of the crippling of his body.

The wind howled at him; his fingers seemed numb in his gloves.

Frostbite – another menace of the serviceman. Men lost fingers and toes to the condition, almost overnight.

Mr Nunn sunk his hands into his pockets and tried to pull himself back to the present, a task that seemed to get harder every time he disappeared into his past. The rain was flying straight into his face, blinding him, but he kept on down the road.

He was doing this for his son. Memories would not stop him from helping his boy.

His son had endured far more than he ever had. His time on the frontline had been cut short by a combination of ill health and exhaustion. His son had served through the entire thing. He told stories that even his father found hard to comprehend despite his own experiences.

His son had served with honour, with courage. But what had that mattered when he came home? Where was the hero's welcome for him?

Mr Nunn had to find a way to make things right. He didn't know how, but he knew he would use his last breath to achieve that goal. Which was why he had turned out on this icy day, forcing himself away from his warm hearth.

How could he enjoy such a luxury as a warm fireside when his son suffered? What was a little walk in the cold after those years in the trenches his Joseph had endured?

He stumbled on, feeling like the only soul out on that miserable morning, though the distant ringing of church bells consoled him that he was not alone in making the effort to leave his comfortable fireside. The Sunday congregations, Catholic and Protestant, would be doing their duty, saying their prayers, singing their hymns.

He hoped that the person he was heading to see was not among them. He had failed to consider that possibility when he had made the decision to seek them out. Too late to turn back now and try another day. He would have to hope his luck held.

He found the street he was looking for, and not long after that he was at the door of a house. He knocked tentatively, fearing he would be rebuffed for disturbing people on a Sunday. He had not thought this matter through, he had been simply so determined to make things right and that had driven him on without a thought to the consequences.

He sniffed, the rain now pouring down his nose. He was ready with an apology when the door was opened by a young man dressed casually as befitted a lazy Sunday. The man looked at him curiously, his eyes asking the question his lips did not.

"Sorry to disturb you on a Sunday," Mr Nunn said, only then becoming aware that his teeth were chattering. "I had hoped to speak to Miss Fitzgerald?"

"You are looking for a detective?" The young man before him smiled. "Unfortunately, my sister is not here. She recently married and now resides with her husband Captain O'Harris. However, I am a partner in her detective business and if you care to speak to me I shall make sure I pass everything on to her. It would be a shame for you to have made a wasted journey.

Mr Nunn shivered in his coat, aware now that rainwater was trickling down the back of his neck.

"Who is it?"

A woman appeared from a doorway that must have led to a kitchen. She had a frown on her face as she looked at him.

"Just someone looking for Clara," the young man at the door called back to the woman.

She headed down the hallway now and gave Mr Nunn an assessing look.

"You look frozen to the bone," the woman spoke. "It must have been important for you to come out on a day like this. You better come in and I shall make you a hot cup of tea."

Mr Nunn was trying to compose himself, having been so afraid a moment ago he would be berated for disturbing the Fitzgeralds on a Sunday, he now found himself stunned by their friendliness.

He remembered his manners and pulled out a hand from his pocket to offer to the gentleman before him.

"Mr Joseph Nunn," he introduced himself.

"Tommy Fitzgerald," Tommy took his hand and shook it. "This is my wife, Annie."

Tommy peered a little closer at the man on his doorstep.

"I served with a Joseph Nunn at the front," he said.

"That would be my son," Mr Nunn explained. "I apologise for disturbing you like this, but I couldn't wait any longer. My son has mentioned you on and off over these last few years. He said you were good friends in the trenches. I read in the paper that your sister, Clara, had become a private detective. I thought if anybody could help us, it would be you."

"Come into the parlour," Tommy said at once. "What has happened to Joseph?"

Mr Nunn entered the house, kicking his feet on the door mat to get off as much of the icy slush on their soles as he could before he stepped further inside. He was so cold that his legs seemed to have gone numb. Tommy took him through into the parlour and settled him before the fireplace, while Annie departed to make tea.

Mr Nunn put out his trembling hands to try to warm them before the fire. The relief of being out of the cold and sitting down reminded him of how unwell he had been lately and brought upon him a sudden heaviness. Only the determination to tell his son's story and ask for help kept him from shutting his eyes at once and succumbing to exhaustion.

"To answer your question, a grave misfortune has happened to my son," Mr Nunn began. "In the late summer of last year, there was a robbery at a local tobacco shop. It was in the papers. You may have read about it?"

Tommy paused for a second to rack his memory. He vaguely thought he had read about it, but it was not something that had particularly caught his eye.

"How does that relate to Joseph?" Tommy asked.

"Joseph had recently begun working at that same tobacco shop," Mr Nunn explained. "When the crime occurred, there was some speculation that it was an inside job, as there was a secret stash of money that was stolen. Apparently the shopkeeper had a special safe beneath the counter where she would keep the nightly takings. She would store these up through the course of the week and then take them to bank. Few people knew about the secret safe, yet when the thief entered the shop, brandishing a pistol, it was the first thing he asked the shopkeeper to empty. The police fancied it meant that someone had inside information. My son had not been working on the day of the robbery and the blame fell upon him. For whatever reason, he chose not to deny the charge, I could never get any information from him on the matter, he became close-lipped on the subject. He ended up being taken to court and found guilty of the crime, though the evidence was slim, and they never did find the missing money.

"The judge looked upon him favourably, nonetheless, perhaps seeing a former serviceman still suffering the effects of the war all these years later. He was only given three months in prison which was a relief for us all, but even so it was more suffering than he deserved. I know he didn't commit the crime. My son has never been a thief."

"I remember Joseph well," Tommy said. "I always considered him an honourable man and a good friend. He always had my back."

"He speaks of you warmly too," Mr Nunn nodded his head. "He always remarked you were a brave and honest man."

Tommy was embarrassed by the praise.

"I don't know about either claim, but I did my best for my regiment."

"It was a difficult time for all the young men who served," Mr Nunn said quietly. "We lost my other son at the front. Joseph made it home, but like so many other young men he wasn't the same person we had wished farewell to all those years before."

"Joseph was a remarkable soldier," Tommy was thinking back to a different time, the familiar maudlin nostalgia fast overcoming him. "I was most proud of him when he earned the Victoria Cross."

"And that brings me to the next part of my sorry tale," Mr Nunn continued. "He earned that Victoria Cross, Mr Fitzgerald, no one can deny the bravery he showed on the day that he was nominated for that award. But under the regulations of the award, a man cannot keep the Victoria Cross if he has done something that would bring dishonour to the holding of such a medal. It is an old regulation, and very few Victoria Cross holders have ever fallen foul of it, but my son is one of them. Not long after his conviction we received a letter from His Majesty himself explaining that my son was to be stripped of his VC. Can you imagine the heartache this gave my boy? He had endured everything else with a calmness that was admirable, but when he learned he was to lose his VC he broke down into tears.

"You have to resolve this for us Mr Fitzgerald. My son is not a thief! I don't know what he is hiding but I am sure of one thing, he is innocent of that crime, and he doesn't deserve to lose his VC because of it."

Tommy hesitated; it was a difficult situation. The police had clearly felt there was enough evidence to arrest and then prosecute Joseph Nunn. Who was he to now question that decision?

It was easy for a father to be blinded by love for a son, and to see what he wanted to see. That Joseph had never denied the crime or tried to defend himself seemed to imply a guilty conscience.

"Were there other suspects for the crime?" He asked.

"None were suggested," Mr Nunn explained. "I always felt that as soon as the police decided my son was responsible, they chose not to look at anyone else. His employer was very quick to point the finger at him."

"And your son has never denied the crime or protested his innocence?"

"Joseph has remained silent on the subject. Only once did I ever get anything out of him when I finally pressed him hard enough to speak. He just said what was the point of saying anything, minds were made-up and that was that."

"I assume he had no alibi for the day of the robbery?"

Mr Nunn frowned at him, not sure what the word meant. Tommy reiterated what he had just said.

"No one knows where your son was on the day of the robbery? There is no one who can state he was with them rather than stealing from a tobacconist?"

"I see what you mean, and no, there was no one who could stand up for him. My son lives alone these days. He likes the solitude. As far as I'm aware there was no one who had seen him that day who could offer him one of these alibis you mentioned."

"That certainly would make things easier for the police," Tommy considered the matter for a moment or two more.

If Joseph was innocent why was he refusing to stand up for himself?

"Will you look into this for us?" Mr Nunn asked him.

"I am willing to do so, but I can make no promises. If your son is refusing to offer an explanation of where he was on that day, or to defend himself, then it will make it very difficult for me to prove him innocent."

"I should have thought that all you needed to do was find the real culprit for the crime?" Mr Nunn gave him a stern look as though he thought he wasn't really trying hard enough.

"Yes, that is the obvious thing to do," Tommy explained carefully. "However, it is not always the easiest, especially with the length of time between the crime and now. Any evidence that might have been present at the scene of the crime will have been lost, and people's memories grow foggy over time."

"You do not inspire hope," Mr Nunn said, bitterness in his tone.

"I merely wish to state the case plainly, so as not to give you false hope. It's about realism rather than giving you fake optimism. On the other hand, I am willing to do everything that I can do to find out the truth of this matter."

"I suppose that is all I can ask of you," Mr Nunn said quietly. "I thought the war had broken my son, Mr Fitzgerald, I thought nothing worse could occur to him. But this situation has virtually destroyed him. Stripping a man of his honour is the worst thing a person can do."

"I understand," Tommy told him gently reaching out a hand to rest lightly on his knee for reassurance. "If you give me Joseph's new address I shall go see him at once."

Mr Nunn was nodding his head and pulling out a piece of paper from his pocket. He had already written out the address in anticipation that Tommy would ask for it.

"I am so very sorry for disturbing your Sunday."

"Nonsense," Annie spoke from the doorway, she was holding a tray of tea things. "We are always here to help people. It sounds like your son has got himself into a serious situation but do not worry, my husband will get him out of it."

Annie looked proudly at Tommy. He inwardly winced at her praise, concerned that she might be overinflating his abilities.

"I will do my best," Tommy said. "As will my sister Clara, who really is the detective around here."

He hoped Clara never got wind of the fact that Annie was now suggesting that he was the detective in the agency rather than her, she might not take to that too kindly.

In fact, her ears might be burning as they spoke.

Chapter Two

Tommy met up with his sister at their shared office the following morning. The office was a small set of rooms above a haberdashery shop. Clara had been renting it since the early days of her career as a private detective in an effort to keep her home life separate from her working life.

It didn't always work as Tommy had discovered the day before with Mr Nunn coming to his home instead of to the office.

Prior to Clara's marriage to Captain O'Harris, Tommy had rarely set foot in her office, he had always seen it as his sister's private space and felt it was wrong to intrude. Tommy considered himself Clara's assistant when it came to the detective business; she assigned him tasks to complete, and he was happy with the arrangement. He was not used to being the one to bring a case to her.

But her time away from the office due to her recent marriage had changed things. People had not stopped coming by with cases, but now they came to him because he was the one in the office. He was starting to think of himself as an actual detective in his own right and it bolstered his confidence. But Tommy was worried how his sister would feel about him taking on cases without her – would she feel he was stepping on her toes?

Clara was already in the office when he arrived. She smiled at him as he entered.

"Good morning, it is a glorious Monday outside."

Clara was quite correct about that; outside the sun had deemed to shine and the sky was a pale blue. It felt like a heavenly promise that soon the winter would be over, and they would trundle back into spring.

"I don't ever recall getting this much post before I was married," Clara added, holding up a pile of envelopes she had just collected from the table. "Has it been like this the entire time I have been absent?"

"More or less," Tommy nodded. "I thought this was the norm for you?"

"Far from it, but it is nice to be wanted," Clara put down the envelopes. "Any urgent cases I should know about?"

Tommy almost jumped as if she had read his mind. Had she surmised he had taken on a case without consulting her first? Why did he feel so guilty about that?

It wouldn't be the first time he had investigated a mystery that someone had brought to him; so why did it feel as though he was keeping secrets from Clara?

"I do have something for us," Tommy said shoving his guilt into a deep place within him and telling himself he was being foolish. "It is somewhat personal to me because it involves someone I served with in the war."

Clara was immediately intrigued; she took the seat behind the desk and motioned for Tommy to take a seat in front.

"How serious is it?" She asked. "Do we need a cup of tea to drink while we brood over the matter?"

"Let me outline it first and then we can decide if the cup of tea is necessary," Tommy smirked, though he was already thinking a cup of tea would certainly be nice after his cold and chilly walk to the office. A blue sunny sky had not made-up for the fact that the temperatures were close to freezing.

"I served in the war with a gentleman called Joseph Nunn," Tommy began. "He was a good soldier, and a good friend to me. We served for quite some time in the same regiment and in the very same platoon. We always had each other's back. After the war was over we lost touch. Really we lost touch after I was injured and invalided out. Joseph wrote to me a couple of times, but I never responded to his letters, I just didn't feel I could. He even offered to come and visit me at home, but I didn't want him to see me, I was ashamed of my useless legs at that time, and I didn't want him to witness me confined to a chair. My own bitterness and shame put a wedge in our friendship and after a while he stopped writing."

"The war made things very difficult for a lot of people," Clara told her brother gently. "You were just simply trying to survive after what happened."

"Maybe," Tommy said solemnly. "But supposing he had needed me after the war? Wasn't it selfish of me to simply cut him off? He might have needed some support from me."

"Whether that is true or not, dwelling on it now will not change what happened in the past. I take it that Joseph Nunn has been back in touch with you?"

"Not directly but through his father," Tommy explained. "That is another reason I feel guilty, I was unaware that Joseph had been accused of robbing a tobacconist's shop. Not only was he accused but he was convicted of the crime and served three months in prison. I was oblivious to the fact that he had been arrested and sent to trial. What sort of friend am I?"

"Friends lose touch from time to time," Clara reminded him gently.

"You didn't deliberately ignore him."

"Didn't I Clara? Because it rather feels as though I did. I must have read about that incident in the papers, I must have seen his name!"

"There is no *must* about it. Supposing it wasn't reported in the paper who had been arrested for the crime? It isn't always the case that a suspect is named. Maybe it was never written down and so you had no way to know it was your old friend who had been accused."

Tommy shook his head, refusing to be excused his neglect of a friend.

"In any case, I have been beating myself up about it all night thinking that I have let Joseph down. Thinking that if I had known sooner, if I had made the connection, that I could have helped him somehow."

"You cannot change the fact that he robbed a tobacconist's shop," Clara pointed out.

"That's just it, Clara. It might not be true that he robbed that shop."

Clara frowned at him.

"What do you mean?"

"His father came to me and said that he believes his son is innocent. He can't explain his belief, and his son has never denied committing the crime, but nonetheless he is certain he did not do this. The evidence against him was flimsy but without Joseph offering a defence it was easy enough for him to be convicted."

"Why would he not deny the crime if he was innocent of it?" Clara said gently to her brother. "I know no one wants to believe it of a former soldier, one who fought bravely for our country, but sometimes people do reckless and unexpected things that are out of character. Maybe he needed the money?"

"No Clara, I refuse to believe that. I can't tell you why I don't believe he did this. It's more a feeling than anything else. But that's by the by, his father wants us to prove his son innocent."

"Yet his son has already been convicted and served a sentence for his crime," Clara pointed out. "Our country's justice system has determined that he was guilty and has punished him as was deemed fit."

"Are you suggesting that our system of justice is never wrong?" Tommy pointed out. "We both know of individuals who have been wrongly accused of a crime. Just because Joseph was committed to trial and found guilty does not mean that he couldn't still be innocent."

"But you just told me he didn't deny the charges, why would an innocent man allow himself to be convicted of a crime he didn't commit?"

Tommy could only shrug at her words.

"I can think of a few reasons, but truthfully there is no point speculating without the facts. The simple truth of the matter is that I'm going to do everything I can to figure out what really happened. I shall discover who really did rob the tobacconist and I will even find out why Joseph allowed himself to be convicted of the crime. This is really important to me Clara, not just because he was a good friend to me, but because he is a man who is truly a hero."

Clara said nothing, it was not her place to question Tommy's convictions. But she knew as well as anyone did that just because a man had served with honour in the war, just because he was a good friend, and a hero, didn't mean he couldn't also end up making bad decisions. Who knew what circumstances Joseph had been placed under at the time of the robbery? Circumstances that forced him into doing something reckless and foolish. It did not make him less of a hero, it just made him very human.

"Well, if we have been tasked with finding out the truth of this case we certainly shall," Clara said to her brother confidently.

Tommy was relieved to hear her words and smiled at her.

"There is something else you should know. Joseph was awarded the VC for his bravery during the war."

"The Victoria Cross?" Clara paused as she took in this information.

The VC was the highest honour a soldier could get for valour in the field. It was sometimes said to be given to the bravest of the brave. It was an award that was not restricted by the rank, age, or class of the recipient, and was an honour that any soldier granted it would be deeply proud of.

"How did he earn the VC?"

"It was in the hellish days of the battle of the Somme," Tommy muttered. "Sometimes it seemed as though the shelling and the shooting were endless, that we would never see the end of it. In the chaos of it all we just had to do our best. Men were going mad from the sheer violence of it all, the sheer chaos and carnage. Half the time when you were trying to cross the front you were walking on the corpses of the dead or having to ignore a hand lifted up as an injured man begged for help. Men were shot to pieces either side of you and you just kept walking, hoping for the best.

"In that slaughterhouse, Joseph proved himself a true hero. Part of our regiment had been sent over the top and we found ourselves surrounded on three sides by German troops. The barbed wire that our shells were supposed to have destroyed was still in place and as we tried to get through it we were being cut down by machine gun fire.

"When it was obvious we weren't going to be able to proceed with so many of our number already having been shot down our commanding officer called for us to retreat. We did so, but it then became obvious that several of those who had been shot down out in No Man's Land were still alive. Joseph wanted to rescue them. It was a risky operation; me and another fellow volunteered to help him and together we traipsed out into the mud, crawling on our bellies to reach each man as best we could. It was impossible to stand up without getting shot. We had to drag the wounded back as best we could while still on the ground.

"We had rescued two men and brought them back like that when I was summoned away for another task. I thought that Joseph would give up trying to get the others back, it was so perilous out there. Horrid thing to say, but you got used to leaving men behind. I had not appreciated Joseph's bravery or his compassion. After I had gone, he went out again by himself. Over and over he dragged a man back to the trenches then went for another. When he was pulling back his fourth man he was shot by a German sniper. The bullet pierced his shoulder, and he barely managed to make it back into the trench.

"Despite bleeding heavily, he was determined to go out again and rescue more, but he was commanded to sit down and have his wounds treated. Not long after that, there was another assault from the Germans and the trench had to be abandoned. Joseph was evacuated along with the wounded men he had saved.

"He did all that without considering there might be some reward for it, he just wanted to try and save as many men as possible. As many of his friends as possible… His gallantry was reported and eventually he was gazetted for the Victoria Cross. He was presented with it at Buckingham Palace by the King. We were all so proud of him."

"What a remarkable gentleman," Clara nodded her head.

"More than remarkable Clara, a good kind man who put others before himself. A man who would never cause harm to someone willingly. I know he felt deep guilt for those he had killed during the war, and for those he hadn't been able to save. That brings me to the second part of this case. Because of his conviction, Joseph had his Victoria Cross removed from him. Not the physical item, but his record of receiving it. The disgrace he felt for this nearly broke him. I cannot let that stand, especially if he is innocent of this crime."

Clara could understand the intensity of Tommy's emotions regarding this case. But she was also trying to be pragmatic about the matter. What possible reason could Joseph have that meant he was willing to accept blame for something he didn't do?

"I have already taken on the case," Tommy said, worried that he had gone over his sister's head. "I hope you don't mind."

"Why would I mind?" Clara asked him.

"Because I didn't ask you first."

"You do not always need to be running around asking my permission to investigate a case," Clara said. "Remember we are partners in this detective business, which means we can work independently when necessary."

Tommy was still somewhat uncomfortable about the situation.

"I don't want you to think that while you were away I just took over the business and made it my own."

"Do you really think I would be so petty?"

"You built this business up on your reputation," Tommy explained himself. "You built it up by proving yourself to be an independent woman, now having your brother involved and people turning to him rather than you, might make it seem as though I have stepped in and taken things over."

"If other people care to see things that way so be it," Clara shrugged. "The people who matter will still understand that I run this business, but that we are partners and that we are fully capable of solving crimes individually if we wish to. For that matter there may come a situation where a gentleman may prefer to speak to a male detective rather than a woman, just as a woman might prefer to speak to a woman detective. Personally, I think we have the best of both worlds between the two of us."

Tommy found himself smiling.

"You really think I could be as good a detective as you?" He asked.

"Well now," Clara smiled at him. "Maybe not *quite* as good as me. I mean I am a natural talent at it. But I am sure you can be pretty good."

"Glad to see you are still humble as always."

"Humble is my middle name," Clara smirked. "And let's not forget that."

Chapter Four

Annie was on a mission of her own.

She had slipped out of the house hoping that no one would notice her or that if they did they would assume she was going about her daily errands. It was not as though anybody was aware that she was involved in her own little game of subterfuge, but from the moment she had decided that she was going to be the undoing of a certain gentleman, so she had begun to feel as though all eyes were upon her.

Mr Maguire had built five bungalows on the clifftop; there was nothing dubious about that as far as Annie knew, but one of the properties had been the unfortunate location for a murder. Mr Maguire was not directly responsible for the incident in his bungalow, but the result for him had been that his properties were now almost unsellable. No one wanted to live in a house where a murder had been committed, and those people who had bought the bungalows either side of the 'death house' – as the papers had so kindly put it – had suddenly found they had cold feet and decided they did not want to be there either.

Mr Maguire had spent a small fortune building the bungalows, hoping that they would make him a hefty return. He was now facing the real possibility of becoming bankrupt all because of something that was out of his control. The person who had brought him into this position was a gentleman who was now awaiting trial for his crimes, but Mr Maguire had focused his attention instead upon Clara and Tommy. Their interference in the mystery of a missing woman had resulted in the discovery that his bungalow was a crime scene. Mr Maguire was convinced that if Tommy and Clara had simply not poked their noses in where they were not wanted, no one would have been any the wiser about the murder, and he could have continued selling on his bungalows without a problem.

The fact that Mr Maguire was essentially placing his own financial future over the apprehension of a murderer didn't even cross his mind. He was sorry that a woman was dead, but he could do nothing about that and why should he suffer when he was very much alive?

Having rationalised all this in his mind, Mr Maguire had then decided to target Clara and Tommy and was currently pursuing them in a case of defamation. He was claiming they had wrongly accused him of committing the murder that had occurred in his bungalow and had gone so far as to besmirch his name by suggesting he had some involvement in the subsequent concealment of the crime.

It was all nonsense of course; Clara and Tommy were not responsible for the rumours that had begun to spread shortly after the discovery of the crime in the bungalow. In contrast, they had done all in their power to prove that Mr Maguire was innocent of the crime. But Maguire saw things differently and, currently desperate for some sort of financial return from his investment, he felt his only solution was to try to get some money out of Clara and Tommy.

There was also a vindictive streak to the man, and he was intent on ruining their careers as private detectives in revenge for what he perceived as their crimes against him. It was a disheartening affair. Clara and Tommy had received papers informing them of the case against them and the date had been set for them to appear in a local civil court. That was not enough for Maguire, who was also now posting information in the newspapers, putting across his side of the story, and making it seem as though Clara and Tommy were up to no good.

The real fear was that even if they won the defamation case, Mr Maguire's attempts to slander them would stick.

Clara and Tommy had opted to pursue the situation in the proper manner by going through the legal courts, employing solicitors, and doing their best to prove their case. In Annie's mind this was all well and good, it was the proper thing to do of course, however she didn't think it was the best solution. She was deeply concerned that the longer Mr Maguire was allowed to continue his campaign against Clara and Tommy the more damage he would do, even if they were eventually proven innocent.

Mud sticks, as the saying goes.

Annie was therefore determined to do something to resolve the matter before it ever got to the courts. What she ideally wanted was for Mr Maguire to make a public apology to her husband and sister-in-law.

Annie was not usually the sort to go into battle; she left all the more confrontational business to Clara and Tommy. She was happier in her kitchen making sure they were well fed and watered. But sometimes you just had to do what you had to do.

That day she was off to meet with Gilbert McMillan, a local journalist who often worked with Clara, (and equally often hindered her) to discuss a plan to solve the Maguire problem.

A few weeks ago, Annie had persuaded Gilbert to help her find something they could use against Mr Maguire. It was nefarious and underhand, Annie admitted, it was also morally dubious. She was essentially asking him to help her commit blackmail.

But she couldn't let Mr Maguire win, it was as simple as that.

Annie set out that morning with her shopping basket over her arm pretending she was doing nothing more than going to buy bread, when really she was meeting Gilbert up at a local teashop to discuss some new information.

Gilbert looked cheery when she arrived at the teashop. He had picked a table at the back, in a corner where it was slightly shadowy. If Gilbert had wanted to make it obvious they were two people meeting up to discuss something secret then the spot he had chosen could not have been better. Annie almost groaned to herself, casting her eyes quickly around the teashop in the hopes that there was no one about she knew. Satisfied that as far as she could tell there was no one who would recognise her, she slipped through the tables and sat herself opposite Gilbert.

Gilbert was an ugly sort of fellow, there was no nicer way of putting it. He had large ears, an ungainly nose, and a narrow face. His hair was always something of a mess and he smoked so heavily that his teeth were stained an unappealing yellow. He looked every inch the journalist and, on the whole, Annie considered him a deeply unpleasant character, though she was prepared to admit there was a well-hidden good side to the man.

After all, he was willing to help her.

Besides, when you needed someone to assist you to uncover dirt on another person, the sort of fellow you were going to have to ask was a chap like Gilbert.

"Would you like a cup of tea?" Gilbert asked as she sat down.

"No, let's just get on with this."

"You look really put out, is it so unsettling sitting with me?"

Gilbert chuckled as he said this.

"You know the answer to that very well."

"Well I suppose I do, but you don't have to say it so sharply," Gilbert attempted to look hurt though it was not a very convincing expression on his face. It took a lot more than a sharp word from Annie to make him feel hurt. "I've been doing some digging as you asked me to, and I think I might have found something that we could use."

Annie was glad that he was getting to business at once; she tried not to look too enthusiastic as he mentioned that he had found out some information for them.

"What have you discovered?" She asked.

"When I was digging into Mr Maguire's financial records I became curious as to where he got the money to fund his bungalow development. Prior to building those properties he had not apparently had any interest in the building market. Then suddenly he seems to get this wad of money and decides to use it to build bungalows."

"What was he doing before he became a housebuilder?" Annie wondered.

"My exact thoughts," McMillan held up a finger to indicate that he had been working on this and then pulled out his notebook. "What I learned pretty quickly is that Mr Maguire has dabbled in a number of business schemes, some of them more legitimate than others and all of them ended up failing. However, through each of these schemes he has been able to stay afloat usually by declaring bankruptcy. His debts have therefore been made null and void, but he has always managed to retain enough money to start himself up in some new business.

"So far I have worked out that he has been a typewriter salesman, an entrepreneur making ladies stockings, a theatrical agent, and, for a brief time, a gentleman who ran a business supplying private cabs to the wealthy. None of these occupations lasted for very long and all of them ended with a huge amount of debt and many people out of pocket, but never Maguire."

"Is that enough to use against him?" Annie asked excitedly.

"Not precisely, because I haven't been able to find anything particularly illegal about Mr Maguire's dealings. It's quite obvious that something is amiss with all this, but without evidence it's all just speculation. However, I think I might have someone I can talk to who could assist us in that regard."

Annie was becoming agitated.

"Who is this person?" She asked. "And why must we both speak to them?"

"Because the lady is doing a good job of keeping her head down and she might not want to talk to me, but you Annie, you have that air of respectability about you."

Annie was unimpressed by his attempt at flattery. Gilbert carried on regardless.

"What I have discovered is that when Mr Maguire was working as a theatrical agent he had a partner, a woman who assisted him in acquiring acts who he later was going to put on the stage. When the theatrical agency failed, many of these performers were left out of pocket, with no one to turn to. It was a terrible time for them all right, but it was equally terrible for the woman who was assisting Mr Maguire. As far as I can see he dealt her a poor hand as much as he had done to those he was supposed to be representing. She lost a great deal of money."

"Why doesn't it surprise me that Mr Maguire would do that to someone?" Annie shrugged.

"The thing is, this lady resides not far from Brighton and if you want to, we could go and visit her. I think she might be able to tell us something useful, however I don't think she will talk to me because I am obviously a journalist. I need someone else, someone who looks honest and decent."

"You need me," Annie said dryly.

"I do indeed. So what do you say?"

Annie considered what he had told her. She had wanted him to investigate, and this was clearly the fruit of his research. It made logical sense for them to both go to this woman and ask her what she knew about Maguire. Annie still hesitated, however. Was this the right thing to do?

"We could be at the woman's house before the end of the afternoon," McMillan pushed her now.

Annie knew he was becoming too involved in the case, but she had wanted him to be keen, knowing it would get him to work faster and swifter. Wasn't this what they all wanted after all?

She drummed her fingers on the table, thinking hard.

"Do you really think this woman will be the key to helping us?"

"It's impossible to say for certain, not without meeting her in person. But I do think it could be hugely worthwhile to speak to her. From everything I have learned I should say the woman has quite the grudge against Mr Maguire."

Annie resolved herself, she had promised to help her family, and she was not going to back out now.

"Very well Mr McMillan we ought to get going at once then."

Gilbert looked delighted that she had agreed. He downed the last dregs of his tea from his cup, slurping in a horrible manner that made Annie cringe.

As they were walking back through the tables to the door of the teashop, Annie suddenly realised there was someone she knew sitting at one of them. Miss Denby was something of an old rival to Annie. They tended to both enter the same cooking competitions, and both were a dab hand at pastry. The last person Annie wanted to see her with Gilbert McMillan (who always looked disreputable no matter what he tried) was Miss Denby. As McMillan held the front door of the teashop open for Annie and motioned her through she felt Miss Denby's eyes on her. She tried not to think about it, but she knew before the evening was out there would be gossip running everywhere about how Annie Fitzgerald had been out with a strange gentleman, one who looked none too salubrious. Annie cringed to herself but what could she do? Sometimes you had to take a bullet for the greater good.

Chapter Five

Tommy and Clara headed for the home of the younger Joseph Nunn. He was the obvious man to speak to as they began their investigation into what really happened at the tobacconist's shop. His father had indicated to Tommy that Joseph was aware his old trench comrade had been asked to investigate his situation. As with everything relating to the crime, he had been noncommittal, almost apathetic, to what was happening.

"What sort of fellow is your friend?" Clara asked her brother as they headed west through Brighton to the house.

Though Clara had full access to her own car, and a chauffeur to drive it, courtesy of Captain O'Harris, they had decided to go on foot that day. Tommy was reluctant to show up at his old friend's home in a chauffeur driven car; it seemed slightly improper. He was worried what Joseph might think seeing him roll up in an expensive car.

Joseph's father had indicated that his son had had difficulty finding work after the war and was struggling financially. That was one of the reasons he had taken the job in the tobacconist shop. It was also the reason that the police thought him a very likely suspect for stealing the money. He had a number of debts that he was desperate to pay.

However, as his father had pointed out, those debts remained unsettled despite the sum he had supposedly stolen, implying that he had not taken it and used it to pay off those people he owed.

This had failed to convince the police, and they had continued to persist in pursuing Joseph, seeing him as their only suspect. His refusal to protest his innocence had gone against him and made it very difficult to mount any sort of defence.

"He is a good man. Honest, hardworking," Tommy said to his sister. "He could make you smile on the gloomiest of days, the sort of chap who's always joking and jesting. And he was brave as hell. Nothing would stop him from reaching a wounded man or claiming a machine gun post if necessary. I remember times in the trenches when we had run out of ammunition and all we had to defend ourselves with was our bayonets. Joseph rallied us and led us into a charge. He was a man to inspire other men."

"He doesn't sound like a fellow who would suddenly decide to rob a tobacconist's shop," Clara remarked.

They were now stepping off the bus and finding themselves in the road where Joseph Nunn lived. He had a room in a small house along a narrow backstreet. The sort of cramped lodgings where you shared a bathroom with the other residents and slept and worked in the same room.

Tommy double checked the address on the slip of paper he had been given by Joseph's father, then strolled up towards one of the houses in the road. There was a small garden in front of the house, though it was more of a yard and barely warranted the name of a garden. The windows had thick net curtains hanging up over them and the door had been freshly painted, suggesting that though this was a humble accommodation it was at least taken care of.

Tommy knocked on the door and they both waited.

"I should have kept in touch with Joseph," Tommy said

thoughtfully. "I owed him that."

"You were in a dark place after the war, don't judge yourself too harshly."

"I was only thinking of myself. I couldn't think of anyone else. What if Joseph had needed me during that time, what if I could have been the friend to him he had been to me?"

"Regret will achieve very little now," Clara reminded him. "We're doing what we can for your friend. This is his hour of need, and we are here for him."

Tommy nodded his head in understanding, though he didn't look entirely convinced.

The door was finally answered by an older woman in carpet slippers and a floral dress. She had her hair swept back under a handkerchief and a cigarette was hanging out of her mouth. She seemed a friendly enough soul, however, and glanced at them with watery eyes, smiling pleasantly.

"If you are looking to sell me something I am sorry, but I don't have the money to spare, and I already have two bibles."

Clara wondered how often Bible salesman came around this neighbourhood; perhaps they thought it was an area that would benefit from sales of the good book.

"We are here to speak with Joseph Nunn," Tommy explained. "He should be expecting us. I am his old comrade from the war. We served together."

The landlady looked Tommy up and down.

"You look as though you made it through the war all right. There is something in the eyes of a man who served," she said. "I will let Joseph know you are here. He hasn't been himself since that awful business, but I suppose you know all about that?"

Tommy didn't want to say that was the reason they were there, so he just murmured that he was aware, and he wanted to check up on an old friend. The landlady departed from the door and headed upstairs; they heard her shuffling along in her slippers. She had left the door ajar and as it was cold they saw no reason not to step inside the house and linger in the hallway.

"Sometimes you look around you and think 'I am only where I am by the grace of God,'" Tommy said nodding his head at their surroundings.

The house was neat and tidy, but it was also well worn. The wallpaper was stained and had turned an unappealing tan colour. The woodwork was worn bare where many feet or hands had rubbed against it and the stair bannisters had a paler patch running in a line along their centre, where palms regularly ran across them. The furniture was all old and tired but still serviceable. The rug beneath their feet looked as though it might only last one more winter, so threadbare in places they could see through it to the floorboards below.

Tommy was thinking how he could easily have ended up in a place like this, or worse, had it not been for the pragmatism of his sister. When their parents had died there had been no income coming into the household other than from the few investments that their late father had made. It was just enough to sustain the house, but it meant there was little extra left over for anything else. The tipping point could easily have been the need to replace a window or to have the chimney swept. Instead of giving up in despair and waiting to see what someone else would arrange for her, Clara had decided that she would be the one to sort things out for the family. Becoming a private detective had not been on the cards immediately but it was something that Clara fell into quite naturally. Because of her work Clara was able to keep the roof over their heads and ensure there was money left over for all the luxuries, extras and emergencies that could come up in life.

Tommy had come home broken and in a wheelchair thinking he would never walk again. He had not dared to imagine in those early days that he might at one point in the future become a detective along with his sister and be able to earn an income himself. Part of the humiliation of being an invalid was not being able to earn money, something that hit a man's pride hard.

Yes, Tommy had fallen on his feet ultimately, and now he could not only support a household for himself and his wife, but he could also say that he was proud of what he did and felt that he was making a difference to the local community. He could not imagine what it would be like to be Joseph, someone who could not even blame the inability to earn money on a war wound, but who rather fell afoul of the economic crisis that had arisen after the war.

There was simply not enough work to go around after the conflict. Despite the decimation of the young male population of Britain, there was still a lack of work for those that returned from the war, whether they had all their limbs or not. It was a hard time for everyone, and as yet things were not picking up.

Tommy's success in the face of Joseph's perceived failure was another reason he was feeling guilty right now. He shuffled his feet and looked uneasily through the open front door at the road beyond. People in shabby workaday clothes were wandering back and forth about their daily tasks. This was a place people struggled every day to earn enough to pay for bread and fuel for the fire.

The landlady appeared on the top of the stairs again and waved at them.

"He says he's ready to see you now," she remarked. "I won't come down again as I want to dust the second room on this floor, and it saves my knees if I don't keep climbing up and down the stairs. Would you mind closing the front door for me?"

They did as she asked and then headed up the stairs. The landlady motioned them to a partly open door on the left of the landing, then she headed to the right. They went through the door and found themselves in a narrow long room with just one window at the front looking out over the street. This room served as bedroom, sitting room, and dining room for Joseph.

They had been incorrect in the assumption he shared bathroom; the only facilities the property had was an outhouse at the bottom of the yard. There was a stand in the room which accommodated a jug of water and a bowl where Joseph could wash himself and shave.

Joseph was stood with his back to them when they arrived, he spun around immediately. He was a tall man – taller than Tommy who was not short by any means – with a square chin and deep brown eyes. His face ought to be handsome as it was well proportioned, but there was something slightly haggard about it, as though time had taken a toll on him that was far greater than it should have been at his age. He smiled when he saw Tommy and held out a hand towards him. Tommy stepped forward, clasped the hand, and shook it heartily.

"I should have called on you sooner Joseph."

"It doesn't matter," Joseph responded patting him hard on the shoulder. "We all came away from those trenches different men."

Tommy's guilt was not immediately assuaged.

"This is my sister, Clara O'Harris. You ought to shake her hand as she only approves of men who shake her hand."

Tommy grinned at his joke.

Joseph took the hint and offered his hand to Clara. She politely shook it.

"It is a pleasure to meet you, Joseph, Tommy has been telling me about you."

"I hope he's not telling you all my secrets," Joseph chuckled. "Some of the stories he has about me ought to only be told in a wartime trench and not in the company of ladies."

"I'm sure there was nothing you did to be ashamed of," Clara responded promptly.

Joseph immediately shook his head, and his smile disappeared.

"There were lots of things that happened out there on the front of which I am deeply ashamed. There is a great deal from that time I would prefer to be completely forgotten."

Clara realised she had made a misstep; she had only meant to suggest that no story that her brother could tell of his friend and their time in the war would shock or disturb her, though truthfully there were plenty of tales she probably would hear that would do just that. However, she had not thought to herself quite how the comment would be taken and now she felt a fool.

"That was a very stupid thing for me to say," Clara replied. "What I meant was you can tell me anything, and I will listen to any story you have to tell. I make no judgement."

Joseph gave her a sad smile but said no more.

"Why don't you both take a seat? I'm afraid there's not much room in here but if you wouldn't mind sitting on the bed?"

Clara and Tommy settled themselves on the bed, while Joseph pulled over a chair that was in the corner of the room and proved to have a wobbly leg. He knew exactly how to sit on it so that it didn't wobble him over onto the floor.

"I know why you are here old chap," he said to Tommy. "But I think it's a wasted journey. The courts decided my fate and I have served my time. Why drag this all up again?"

"Because your father believes you are innocent," Tommy stated.

Joseph pulled a strange face; it seemed partly amusement, partly annoyance.

"You know how it is, old man, my father cannot bring himself to believe his son has descended into crime. But such is life."

"You pleaded guilty to your crimes?" Clara now asked.

"Because I was guilty," Joseph shrugged.

But Clara noticed that he couldn't meet her face when he said this. She found that very interesting.

"I was sorry to hear they took away your VC," Tommy remarked. "They shouldn't have done that."

"Well they didn't actually take the VC itself away. I still have it with me. However the record of my receiving it has been eradicated and there was a notice placed in *The Gazette* to state that I had been stripped of the honour. It did break my heart."

"It is not fair to do that to an innocent man," Clara said to him quietly.

Joseph didn't look up at her, keeping his head down, his gaze on his hands.

"Because you are innocent, aren't you Joseph?" Clara persisted.

Joseph refused to speak, instead picking at his fingernails in an agitated fashion.

"We want to help you," Tommy added.

"There is no help for me now, old man. Don't poke your nose into this. I'm not worth the trouble."

"I refuse to believe that," Tommy said firmly.

"A lot has changed since the war," Joseph said sadly. "I don't think I am the man you remember me as Tommy. I am sorry. But I can't change what I did. Sometimes life doesn't quite work out the way you expected it to."

Chapter Six

Much to Annie's surprise Gilbert McMillan turned out to have his own motor car.

It was not one of the big contraptions that she had become familiar with through Captain O'Harris, but it was a sufficient machine to take two people from one place to another.

"I had not realised it was so lucrative being a journalist," Annie remarked as Gilbert drove them along the roads towards a nearby village where the woman they wanted to question resided.

"Are you referring to the car?" Gilbert asked her grinning from ear to ear. "It was my little gift to myself. I saved up for two years. It saves a lot of walking and means I can get to stories quicker than ever. Though the downside is it does breakdown fairly regularly and I had to become something of a mechanic to manage it all."

Annie reached up to make sure her hat was still in place. Gilbert drove quickly and the vehicle did not have side windows; the great gusts of wind that kept driving through the car threatened to take her hat clean off. She was not convinced this was a nicer form of travel than being on the local omnibus, which *did* have proper windows and where one could sit without fear of being blown about or getting wet.

"The lady we are going to see is called Miss Pendleton," Gilbert now informed her as they drove along country lanes.

He seemed to know exactly where he was going and didn't refer to a map even once. Annie began to wonder if he had been to this woman before.

"Miss Pendleton inherited a small fortune from her late grandparents and part of this was what she invested in the business with Mr Maguire. It was deeply unfortunate that the whole thing went bust, it seems that she lost a considerable fortune in the matter."

"And I assume she is not friendly towards Maguire these days?" Annie asked him.

"Definitely not," Gilbert replied. "When I made contact with her asking if we could come over and see her, and I explained that we were looking for further information on Maguire's business dealings, she immediately wanted to talk. I made it plain that we were not on Maguire's side and were looking for potential scandal relating to him. She seemed most eager to speak to us."

"Well, you know what they say about a woman scorned."

"Miss Pendleton is certainly that woman," Gilbert nodded his head. "I'm just hoping that she is able to give us the information we need."

They had emerged from the country roads into a small, quiet village. Annie had failed to glimpse its name on a roadside sign as they had driven through. It was one of those tiny, out-of-the-way places that was really just a road with a few houses either side. Probably everybody knew everybody else, and more than likely most were related to each other. She noted that one of the properties was a general shop that sold everything from sewing thread to fresh fruit, next door to it was a butcher. She could smell fresh bread baking in the air which suggested there was a bakery somewhere nearby that she had yet to spot. The village's high street was quiet at this time of year, as there was not much need for people to be wandering about in the cold and the wet. There was, however, a gentleman with a horse stood to one side. A cart attached to the horse was loaded with what appeared to be milk urns.

Gilbert was at last looking as though he was unsure of where he was going. He pulled the car to a stop and headed over to the gentleman with the milk cart. Annie watched him from a distance trying to get a feel for this place and wondering about Miss Pendleton.

What sort of woman would she be? Annie did not regularly go around visiting strangers; she was not like Clara who would happily speak to anybody without a care. Truthfully, Annie was nervous. She was wondering how Miss Pendleton would react to them.

She was beginning to regret leaving Brighton.

"The milkman says we need to go to the end of this road and turn left," Gilbert said when he returned to the car. "There is a turning that we must follow that takes us to a little old cottage where Miss Pendleton lives."

Without another word he slipped the car into gear, and they drove off. At the end of the village high street they spotted the left turning that the milkman had mentioned. It took them down a rutted lane which was more used to carts and horses than it was to cars. Annie bumped up and down in her seat as Gilbert drove in what she fancied was too great a haste. They spied the cottage on their right. It was set a short distance back from the lane with a small patch of garden around it which was no doubt picturesque and beautiful in the summer. Whoever owned the property clearly took good care of their garden and she noted that some of the more delicate plants had been wrapped in potato sacks to protect them from the frost, while the flower beds had been carefully weeded and a greenhouse was just visible at the back of the property.

Gilbert pulled the car up to a halt beside the garden gate.

"We shall have to hope no one comes down this lane," he remarked with a laugh.

His car was completely blocking the lane, which was only wide enough for a single vehicle, but the notion that he might inconvenience someone coming down the lane amused rather than worried him.

Annie descended from the car saying no more to Gilbert, it would be his problem if someone got upset that his car was in the way.

Gilbert led the way up the garden path towards the cottage. He was preening himself as he went, adjusting his collar, running a hand through his hair in an attempt to make it look less like a haystack and doing all in his power to look somewhat respectable. Annie didn't like to say it aloud, but she fancied he was failing in his efforts. Gilbert looked every inch exactly what he was – a nosy, morally questionable, journalist.

There was something about Gilbert that meant he always looked sleazy. As if you knew just by looking at him, he couldn't keep a secret and would use anything he heard to make a good story. Try as hard as he might, he just always looked villainous. Annie wondered what people must think of her tagging along with him? Surely she looked out of place beside the weaselly journalist? At least she *hoped* she looked out of place and people realised she was eminently more respectable than Gilbert.

Before they had reached the door of the cottage, it had been opened by an older woman who stood on the doorstep with her arms folded across her ample bosom. The lady had bobbed hair that was a soft brown colour, and it framed her round face. She was in her forties and the fashions of the day were not favouring her plump figure. However, she was doing her best to pull them off, and the green, straight-waisted dress she was wearing was obviously of the latest design. Annie fancied she would do better to pick clothes that matched her figure, but she knew how hard it was to go against the fashions of the day, and to try to be your own woman.

Miss Pendleton didn't look entirely pleased to see them.

"Gilbert McMillan, dear lady," Gilbert stepped forward and gave a polite bow to Miss Pendleton. "May I introduce Annie Fitzgerald, my assistant."

Annie nearly swung her shopping basket straight at Gilbert. His assistant! How dare he even suggest such a thing! But she could hardly have an argument with him on the matter while stood in front of the woman who they wished to interview. She kept her mouth shut but cast Gilbert a fierce glare.

"I've been expecting you," Miss Pendleton said in a voice that was far from welcoming. "You best both come in."

She stalked into the house, and they followed her. She showed them through to a comfortable sitting room. A sofa was set before the window and caught what little sunshine was available that day. A fire was burning warmly in the hearth opposite, and a large ginger cat was stretched out on the rug taking full advantage of the heat. Miss Pendleton motioned for them to sit down on the sofa and took an armchair to one side, there was a bag of knitting just beside it which she moved out of the way as she sat down.

"I know you are here to talk about Mr Maguire, so let's be getting on with it."

The woman was both brusque and fearsome. Annie wondered what they were going to achieve speaking to her.

"As I mentioned in our earlier correspondence," Gilbert began, apparently not put off by the woman's demeanour, "Mr Maguire is causing problems for certain people in Brighton, and we are looking into the matter. I am curious about his previous business dealings, especially seeing how all of them failed so dramatically, yet he managed to have enough income left over from them to purchase land and build five bungalows."

"Bungalows he cannot now sell," Miss Pendleton smiled smugly to herself.

"Indeed, that's true," Gilbert nodded his head. "But I want to talk about his business dealings before that, especially his business dealings involving you."

"I should never have become involved with him," Miss Pendleton huffed to herself. "I should have realised he was simply a charmer from the moment I set eyes on him. But he had me under his spell all too quick. Before I knew it, I was agreeing to assist him in his theatrical agency. He sold it to me as the perfect investment, no risk attached at all. He would find the talent and make sure that they were taken on at various theatres and I would just sit back and watch the money roll in."

"I take it that didn't happen?" Annie asked quietly.

A moment later she wished she had not asked, as Miss Pendleton's terrible gaze fell upon her, and she felt herself shrinking back from it. Miss Pendleton was not a woman you crossed. She was amazed that Mr Maguire had dared to do so.

"I realised too late what a fraud he was," Miss Pendleton remarked. "I am not so easily fooled, and I am still ashamed that he took me in. His business arrangements were flawed from the very start. He did not know the theatre business as he had sworn he did to me. He did not have the contacts he needed to ensure that his acts got on the stage. Within a year of starting up the theatrical agency, it was quite obvious that he was struggling. I have seen no return on my investment, and I wrote him a letter demanding to have my money back. That was when he responded telling me he was declaring bankruptcy and there was no money to return.

"I was absolutely furious, and I did what I could via my own solicitors, but they informed me there was nothing to be done. There was simply no money to return to me. I was left out of pocket and, even worse, Mr Maguire had given my name to those acts he was supposed to be representing, saying that I would be a person to contact to deal with their future arrangements. I ended up with a load of people on my doorstep demanding to know why they had no engagements, and where their money was going to come from."

"Your solicitors could not find out what had happened to the money?" Gilbert asked.

"Whatever had occurred to it, it had disappeared and there was no trace of it," Miss Pendleton shook her head. "Yet, barely a month after the bankruptcy was declared and finalised, Mr Maguire reappears running a different business. I cannot say where he got the money to begin this business from. Maybe he found someone else stupid enough to invest in him, or maybe he didn't lose my money as he stated and hid it somewhere to use to fund his new venture. Whatever the case I was out of pocket, and he was clearly flourishing."

Miss Pendleton shook her head sadly.

"I invested that money hoping it would make me a nice return for when I am in my old age. The money I inherited is not endless. I was trying to provide for myself, to make sure I had a secure future. Instead I made my future even worse. My savings are all gone and all I can do is hope to find a way to turn things around at some point."

Miss Pendleton sighed and looked around her sitting room. Annie could imagine she was thinking about the possibility of losing this cottage, of having to move somewhere else. She felt sorry for the woman.

"Mr Maguire sounds like a con artist," Annie said firmly. "All these business ventures he has started and then has abruptly finished, isn't that how a con works?"

"A very good point Annie," McMillan grinned at her. She wondered when he had decided it was ok for him to call her Annie. "I think we could be on to something here."

"If that is the case then are the bungalows just the next stage of his con tricks?" Annie speculated.

"That is certainly something to consider," Gilbert nodded enthusiastically. "Is there anything else you could add Miss Pendleton which might offer us a way to find out something further about Mr Maguire's activities?"

Miss Pendleton considered this for a moment, tapping one finger on the arm rest of the chair she was sitting in. By the fireplace, the ginger cat flicked its tail almost in rhythm to her tapping.

"I don't know if it is relevant," she finally spoke. "But there was a man who I used to see quite often when I visited Mr Maguire's offices. During the first few months I would regularly pay calls upon Mr Maguire to see how everything was going. This gentleman was nearly always present, but he would excuse himself the second I arrived. There was something shifty about him, something I didn't quite like. I did once ask Mr Maguire who his visitor was. He simply smiled at me, 'you mean Mr Mullins? He is nobody, do not think about him.' That was all he ever said, but I am sure of this, Mr Mullins was not simply a nobody. Unfortunately, I cannot tell you what exactly his involvement with Maguire was or if it will do you any good chasing him up."

Chapter Seven

After their visit with Joseph, Clara and Tommy next headed to the tobacconist's shop where the robbery had occurred.

The lack of details they had learned from speaking to Joseph had caused them to think that there was more to this story than they had yet to discover. He was far too willing to accept the blame for the robbery, yet he did not seem the sort of man who would commit such a crime. In Clara's experience, robbers and burglars were not the sort of self-effacing individuals Joseph Nunn presented himself as, who would simply admit their guilt and accept all the consequences that followed. Equally, there was something curious about the fact that the money had not been used to clear Joseph's debts.

If he had stolen the cash to help himself out of a hole, why had he not used it?

The proceeds of the robbery had just disappeared. The police had never found the money despite thoroughly searching Joseph's room and going through all his personal belongings.

In short, Clara was convinced there was more to this story than she was being told.

The tobacconist's shop was in West Street, a small corner shop with dark wood facade and gold lettering on the windows that stated what it sold. There was a display of fancy cigar boxes in one of the windows, advertising that they were from Cuba. The images on the front showed wealthy gentlemen smoking the cigars while being waited on hand and foot by what appeared to be native servants.

Clara was not sure what to make of the pictures, especially as in the background she thought she noticed some rather scantily clad ladies. There was something about them that was unsettling, perhaps it was the way that the servants had been painted looking as though they were more slaves than paid help.

They entered the tobacconist's shop and were immediately assailed by the combined scents of various tobacco leaves. Though the shop front was strictly a no smoking area – there was a room at the back where people could sample the tobacco on sale – there was still a strong aroma from the various tobacco leaves. Some smelt sweet, others almost had a coffee-like hint to them. Clara reflected that it was actually a rather pleasant smell; a lightly aromatic and harmonious aroma. She was not a smoker herself and had never been inclined towards taking up the habit, but she could appreciate the organic scent of the tobacco all around her.

Behind a counter at the back of the shop stood a woman. She was in her late fifties and worn a light dress with a cardigan pulled around her shoulders though her arms were not through the sleeves. She was thin in the sort of way that could easily make her look haggard as she got older. There was already a certain boniness about her joints that made her look older than she probably was. She had a small pair of glasses perched on her nose and her hair, which was rapidly turning grey, had been swept up into a scraggly bun.

She glanced up as the bell over her door rang and smiled at them gently, clearly anticipating they were customers.

"Good morning, my name is Clara O'Harris," Clara immediately introduced herself. "This is my brother Thomas Fitzgerald. We are here because we wanted to ask you some questions about the robbery that occurred in your shop not so long ago."

The woman looked at them in some surprise, her smile faded.

"That happened last year, and it is all over and done with. The culprit was immediately discovered, arrested, and has subsequently served a prison sentence for what occurred. I do not wish to go on about the matter any further. I have already forgiven him for what he did, no doubt there were circumstances behind it of which I was unaware."

"That is all very well, but certain things have come to light that are now causing people to question his guilt," Clara fudged around the truth. "It is possible that an innocent man has been disgraced and served time for a crime he did not commit."

"He pleaded guilty to the charges," the woman behind the counter said, looking confused.

"He did indeed," Clara concurred. "However we think he might be protecting someone. I wanted to ask you more about the robbery if I could?"

"I am not sure I want to discuss it," the lady was somewhat abrasive towards them. "I have already spoken to the police long enough about this."

"The police had a different objective to us," Clara put on her most appealing voice. "The police don't always have the resources to dig into a matter as deeply as I am able to. We will try not to take up too much of your time, but we would really appreciate it if you would talk to us about what occurred."

The woman looked ready to refuse to speak to them. At that moment, a man emerged from the backroom. He was tall, wearing a sweater and grey trousers, aged probably in his late twenties or early thirties, making him around the same age as Tommy. His features, though slightly squarer and more robust, mirrored that of the woman at the counter and indicated they were related.

"Anything the matter, mother?"

"Nothing to concern yourself about, Stuart," the woman turned to her son and shooed him back into the room he had appeared from. "I shall handle this, go back to what you were doing."

The young man took a closer look at Clara and Tommy, as if wanting to imprint their faces onto his memory. He had dark hair and slightly narrow eyes that made it look as though he was squinting all the time. Otherwise he had quite an innocuous face, not one that you would define as either handsome or ugly, rather one that you would simply forget about. After another moment, he turned away and walked into the back room, they heard a door closing behind him.

"Your son is protective of you," Tommy observed.

"He is all I have since the war took my husband from us," the woman responded sharply. "It is only natural for a son to want to keep an eye on his mother in such circumstances."

"Yes, the war cost us all an awful lot," Tommy nodded his head. "I served in the army, and we lost both of our parents during the war."

The woman's stern expression faded a fraction.

"I am sorry to hear that, so many people we valued were taken from us too soon. This was my husband's shop, and I kept it going after he departed as much to honour his memory as because it was a necessity."

"Joseph Nunn also served in the war," Tommy reminded her. "He served with me, in fact. It is not overexaggeration to say that he saved my life more than once. He is a hero who earned the VC, and I am very troubled by the fact that he has now lost that honour because he was accused of this crime. I knew him in the worst period of my life, and he did not strike me as a man who would ever rob a woman or anyone else for that matter."

The woman behind the counter was beginning to look more and more uncomfortable.

"I never accused him you know," she said now clasping her hands together. "I never accused anyone. I reported the crime to the police as one is expected to, and they took it from there. I was most surprised when they told me they had arrested Joseph for the crime. He hadn't been working here very long, but I had always considered him a decent fellow. He had been reliable, and I had no reason to doubt him. But then he pleaded guilty to the crime, and I supposed that I had just been very misguided."

"What if you were not misguided," Clara suggested to her. "What if he took the blame so that someone else was not accused of the crime?"

"Surely that is a remarkable thing for anyone to do?" the woman shook her head.

"People do it all the time," Tommy remarked. "During the war it was almost commonplace for people to sacrifice themselves for each other. For a man like Joseph, that mentality would have survived the war and come home with him. He is the sort of man who would be prepared to lose his own honour to protect someone else's."

The woman behind the counter was beginning to look uneasy; she rubbed her thumbs over the top of each other as she considered what they were saying.

"I was upset when the police arrested Joseph. I thought that perhaps I had been misguided when I had picked him. For so many years I refused to have an assistant in this shop, aside from my own son, simply because I didn't feel I could trust anyone. But I have grown old, and my health is not quite what it used to be. My doctor told me that I ought to employ someone so that I might be able to rest more. You see, my son is studying to become an engineer, he wants to move away from the world of shopkeeping. He could no longer help me in the shop for so many hours as he is absorbed in his studies. It became essential I find someone else.

"However, I was uncomfortable about the situation right up until the moment that Joseph came into my shop and said he had seen my advertisement in the window. He explained that he was looking for work, that he had served in the war and was struggling to find any long-term occupation. He showed me his credentials and references and I was satisfied that he seemed to be both hard working and honest. I was so heartbroken when I heard the police had arrested him, it made me doubt my own abilities to pick out a decent person."

"Maybe you were not mistaken?" Clara suggested. "Why don't you tell us exactly what happened the day of the robbery?"

The woman considered what they had told her for a moment or two. It was clear that she had been deeply upset when she had discovered that Joseph was the man behind the robbery of her shop. It had gone deeper than just feeling betrayed, she had felt her pride had been tarnished because she had been so misguided about the young man. For the longest time she had wished that it had not been the case that Joseph had robbed her, she had wished that the police had got it wrong.

Now here was the possibility that she had been right all along. There had always been an unsettling notion at the back of her mind that something didn't quite fit about Joseph being a thief. Now Clara was making her wonder if her doubts had been correct.

"I will tell you all I know, and you can make a decision from that," she declared to them.

"That is all we can ask," Clara smiled at her.

"It was Thursday afternoon when it occurred," the woman began. "It was not long before closing time and I was here by myself. A gentleman came in through my door. It was a cold day, and I was not surprised to see that he was well wrapped up, he had on a long coat with the collar pulled up and he had a scarf around his face covering everything apart from his eyes. His hat had been pulled down virtually to his ears. He had his hands in his pockets, which I just assumed was because he was cold, but when he came to the counter he pulled his hand out of his pocket, and he had a pistol in it which he pointed at me. I almost had a heart attack right there and then! I threw up my hands and took a step back from the counter. In a gruff voice he demanded I give him all the money from my secret safe. I didn't even argue with him, I did exactly what he wanted. I wasn't to know if the gun was loaded or not, or whether he would actually shoot me. All I knew was that I wanted him out of the shop as quickly as possible. I didn't even question how he knew about my secret safe.

"I took out the money, bundled it up and handed it over to him without a word. He said nothing to me, just took the money, walked backwards for a few paces with the gun still trained on me, then slipped out the door. That was it, truthfully I didn't expect the police to do anything much about it or to ever find the culprit. As soon as he was gone, and I was sure he was nowhere to be seen, I dashed out into the road and called out for a policeman. As it happened there was a constable not far away patrolling the beat and he came running over. I told him what had happened and not long after that a police inspector came and interviewed me about the matter. That was the first time I really considered that the man had asked about my secret safe, the one only certain people know about.

"The police inspector said that could be an important clue. He went away with this information and a list of people who had worked for me in the past, not that that was very long and of course Joseph's name was right at the top. It took me by surprise when he came back only a day later and informed me that Joseph had admitted to his crime, and they were going to arrest him."

"What sort of gun did he point at you?" Tommy asked, thinking such a detail could be important.

The woman glared at him.

"It was a small gun. The sort of thing people brought back from the war. I wasn't exactly paying much attention to what make it was."

Clara changed the topic, hoping to calm the woman.

"You said that you have employed other people in the past?" Clara asked the woman.

"As I mentioned before, I am not inclined to have any assistance here in the shop," the woman explained with a hint of pride. "However, when my husband was alive he often employed a Saturday boy to make deliveries for him. I gave the police the names of those who I remembered, just in case one of them might have come back all these years later to rob the secret safe. It's been there since my husband's day you see; he was the one that started the practise."

"Did the police follow up on any of these other names?" Clara asked her.

The woman simply didn't know and shook her head.

"I am telling you all I know. I was surprised as anybody else that Joseph was the one accused of this crime," the woman paused for a moment. "You know, it would be a great relief to me if you discovered he was innocent. I know it sounds foolish, but it would make me feel better about my own ability to judge a person's character."

"Thank you for taking the time to talk to us," Clara smiled at her. "Whatever happens, we will be sure to keep you informed."

At that moment, behind them, the door of the shop opened and the bell above it rang. The woman had a new customer, and they departed discreetly to leave her in peace. They now had something to go on and it was time to go to the police station and see what information they had gathered on the crime. Clara knew the inspector would not be happy about the fact that she was investigating a case that he considered closed and for which a suspect had already been convicted of the crime. But what other choice did she have? If there had been a question of injustice then someone had to make things right, and at that moment in time the only person Clara could see doing that was her.

Chapter Eight

They made their way back towards the police station, taking advantage of a bus that was passing through West Street just as they were leaving the tobacconist's shop. Clara was hoping she could avoid Inspector Park-Coombs, at least until she had some evidence that Joseph had been wrongly convicted. Though they had a pretty sound working relationship, it never paid to tread on each other's toes.

The bus dropped them off not far from the police station and as they entered they were warmly greeted by the desk sergeant.

"And what can I do for you today?" He asked them.

"I was hoping to be able to look at a case report from last year," Clara explained to him.

The desk sergeant asked her for some details about the case she was interested in and when Clara said it was the tobacconist shop robbery from the previous year he stopped immediately.

"The inspector won't like you poking around in that one."

"Why?" Clara asked.

"Well, because it was such an easy case for him to get resolved. One of the few times that the Chief Constable actually praised him for solving a crime. He won't be happy if you now prove something was awry with his conviction."

"I cannot help that. If an injustice has occurred, I simply have to expose it and put it right. I cannot be held responsible for the inspector's feelings."

"I'm just warning you," the desk sergeant informed them.

He then rummaged in a drawer and pulled out a key that was labelled for the police archives. There was a small room at the back of the station which housed an array of records that could be accessed at any point by the police. It was usually in some degree of disorder as there was no one to really keep track of it, but a long time ago Clara had been given permission to access it whenever she wanted to. The records that were held there were only the most recent ones; each year the oldest records were removed and placed in another holding facility for future reference. However, as the robbery had happened so recently, there should be no issue in finding the report on it.

"I don't know what you hope to find, but tread lightly."

With these final words the desk sergeant allowed them to get on with their investigating. They headed down a corridor and towards the small archives room. It was always bursting at the seams with too many case reports and not enough space to store them all.

When they entered the room they found that they had it to themselves. Clara knew that there was a rough sort of sorting system in use in the archives. She went immediately to the shelves marked 1923 and began looking through them. Reports were supposed to be arranged in alphabetical order, based on a name in the case. However, every policeman who filed a case here had a different opinion on whether they filed it by the victim or the criminal's surname. Some didn't even bother with using a name at all and catalogued a case under R for robbery or under A for armed robbery. The result was a haphazard filing system that would have left the average librarian crying out for a card catalogue.

Despite the chaos, Clara and Tommy were eventually able to find the cardboard folder that contained the report they wanted. It was a dishearteningly slim file, though Clara was not entirely surprised at the sparsity of documents relating to the robbery. They took the folder over to a table that was crammed into a corner and flicked it open.

The first document was a statement typed up by the inspector which basically repeated what they had already been told by the woman at the tobacco shop. Next came the list of names she had given the police of those who had formerly worked in her shop. Clara copied the list into her own notebook, noting that the police had not bothered to interview any of the men on the list, though a few had a notation beside their names in a different hand that read 'deceased.' Clara could only assume that those particular men had perished in the war. They would have been about the right age to have served.

After the list there was a report from the inspector describing how he had spoken to Joseph, and he had admitted to the crime. That was followed by a typed-up confession signed by Joseph. Clara carefully read through it.

"Interesting," Clara said as she went over the statement. "In this paper Joseph mentions nothing about a gun."

"Maybe he considered it an inconsequential detail," Tommy said, reluctant to offer the explanation as he wanted his friend to be innocent, but he had just read through the confession, and it was making him feel as if he had been betrayed himself.

The bluntness of the statement had brought the reality to him. Joseph had been pretty open about everything. He informed the police that he knew exactly where the secret safe was and that Thursday was the best time to rob the shop because that would be when the safe was at its fullest.

"He simply states that he walked into the shop demanded the

money took it and left," Clara persisted. "He barely mentions the fact that he had a scarf around his face. The lack of details has me wondering, was he perhaps just mentioning what he thought the police wanted to hear?"

"You still think Joseph could be innocent, then?" Tommy asked her.

"This confession actually makes me feel more confident of his innocence," Clara replied. "Don't give up hope Tommy, we have barely begun our investigation, and we have a lot of suspects to consider. We shall start with this list of names and see where it takes us."

Chapter Nine

Gilbert drove Annie back into Brighton. Since they did not have an address for the mysterious Mr Mullins, Gilbert decided to use all his resources as a journalist to try and locate him. He pointed the car in the direction of the offices for the *Brighton Gazette* and before long they were sitting outside the building. Gilbert was gracious enough to exit the car first and open the passenger door for Annie; he even offered her his hand. Annie declined to take it but was glad to see he was displaying some manners.

Maybe there was hope for him yet.

Inside the *Gazette* offices, Gilbert showed Annie directly through to his own unkempt desk. Annie flinched as she looked at the heaps of paper, discarded apple cores, pencil shavings, discarded inky typewriter ribbons and other items that had been strewn across his work surface. The only thing missing was an ashtray filled with cigarette ends, and that was because Gilbert had once managed to set fire to his own desk and was now forbidden to smoke inside the office. Admittedly, the other desks around Gilbert's were not much better – all of them seemed to be stacked with paperwork – however, Gilbert seemed to have a knack for collecting all sorts of extraneous rubbish upon his desk that created an impressive heap of debris.

Annie wondered if the office had a cleaner, and if the poor woman ever managed to sweep around Gilbert's desk or had given up the task as simply pointless.

Gilbert had not noticed her disapproval and was searching through the drawers of his desk, pulling out more papers and tossing them around in a haphazard fashion. Annie caught hold of one that nearly fell on the floor and glanced at its heading. It was a reference piece for a story on depleting fish stocks around Brighton's coast and didn't seem relevant to the matter at hand.

"May I ask what you are looking for?"

"I have an index of names in here, somewhere," Gilbert told her. "Anytime I hear a name in relation to a story I file it away in this particular index book so that if I ever need to look it up in the future I can. I thought I would see if I ever wrote down the name Mullins. If that fails us, we'll just have to go to the usual method of looking him up in the Brighton street directory."

"And hope that there aren't that many Mullins living in Brighton," Annie understood what he was attempting to do. "But even if you do have a Mr Mullins listed in your name index, what is to say it is the same Mr Mullins who knows Mr Maguire?"

"I look at it this way Annie, if Mr Maguire is up to something illegal or at the very least immoral, then so is this Mr Mullins, and that means he's potentially been caught up in some other underhand business in the past. My index contains the names of people who I've heard of in relation to another story. If his name has ever been mixed up with something criminal, then I would have made a note of it in my index book. Therefore, there is a good likelihood that if Mr Mullins is listed here, he is the same man who was helping Mr Maguire."

Annie considered this questionable logic, but she didn't say anything and allowed Gilbert to get on with his frantic rummaging through the drawer. After a while she decided she could really benefit from a cup of tea and started to look around the office in the vain hope that someone might be able to prepare her one, or at the very least that there was a stove and a kettle where she could prepare her own.

"Ah, here it is right at the bottom."

Gilbert dragged out a large ledger with a marbled cover. He dumped it on the desk and brushed some dust off its edges.

"I knew I had it in here somewhere," Gilbert smiled.

He flicked open the book and quickly scrolled to the M section. Annie noticed there were quite a lot of names in the book, which was somewhat unsettling. She wondered whether her name featured in there at all, or, for that matter, whether Clara and Tommy were mentioned.

"Aha! I knew it," Gilbert pointed to a line of text on a page. "Here we go, I have listed Mr Mullins as being involved in a scandal concerning the sale of fake coupons."

"You think it might be the same Mr Mullins?" Annie asked.

"Well, I cannot say for certain, but it seems to me that this is just the sort of fellow who would get involved with a man like Mr Maguire. Wait a moment, I shall try and find the article I wrote about the coupon scandal. I always make a little reference in my book next to a name if there is an article about the person."

Gilbert made a note of an index number then excused himself and headed through a door at the back of the office. Annie took a deep breath and remained where she was, trying to ignore the sense of apprehension that was creeping over her. This matter was becoming much more complicated than she had anticipated. In her mind, she had thought they would just give Mr Maguire a stern talking to, and he would then stop all this nonsense with the defamation case.

Was it right that they were poking around in Mr Maguire's past like this?

Then she thought about Miss Pendleton, and how she had been used by Maguire. As someone who had never been involved in business, she didn't fully understand all the ins and outs behind Maguire's betrayal of Miss Pendleton, but she did appreciate that the woman had been mistreated by him.

Did that make him a scoundrel? Probably.

Did that mean she should be digging around in his affairs?

Of that she was not so sure.

Gilbert seemed to be gone for ages, long enough to give Annie a chance to start tidying up his desk. She had already removed all the old apple cores and several pencils that had been sharpened down to mere stubs, along with various piles of shavings from sharpening those same pencils by the time he returned.

"I think I have something Annie, look," Gilbert said enthusiastically.

He showed Annie a piece of paper that he had removed from the archives, it was a typed proof copy for an article that had run in the newspaper. Annie took it to read:

The fake coupon scandal continues to rock Brighton. After it was revealed that a number of fake coupons offering discounts on various wholesale products such as bread cheese and milk were being issued in the town and people were buying them under the impression that they were going to be saving money, we now have further information to reveal on the matter. One lady, who did not wish to be named, confirmed that she had received her coupons from a gentleman by the name of Mr Mullins. He had informed her that by investing a small amount of her money on the book of coupons she would overall be saving a great deal of money on her future groceries. The lady trusted Mr Mullins and fancied that the coupons looked genuine and so purchased a booklet of them using the last of her housekeeping money. When she then tried to redeem the coupons at various grocery stores throughout the town she discovered that they were fake. None of the grocers she spoke to had heard of the scheme and would not redeem her coupons. When the lady tried to find Mr Mullins again to demand her money back she discovered the address he had given to her for his office did not exist.

This is just the latest incidence in the town of booklets of coupons being sold under false promises of saving the customer money. The police are endeavouring to catch up with the culprit, but at this moment in time no arrests have been made. It is therefore necessary for us to inform the general public that if anyone offers to sell them booklets of coupons that will save them money on their groceries, they should immediately turn the offer down.

"He certainly sounds like a person of a similar nature to Mr Maguire," Annie remarked after she had finished the article. "Maguire is also very good at setting up schemes that sound legitimate but that end up leaving people out of pocket."

"I have seen this before," Gilbert nodded his head. "These men set up one business after the other, each one barely legal but doing just enough to avoid getting them into trouble. They get people to either invest in the business or pay for goods and services, and then they either disappear or the business suddenly goes bankrupt."

"But where would the bungalows fit into this?" Annie wondered. "The bungalows are clearly not fake."

"That does raise some interesting points," Gilbert nodded his head. "Why has Mr Maguire gone from schemes that he can slip away from easily to something more concrete? There must be a scam here somewhere, I don't believe he's suddenly become a legitimate businessman, not after what we have learned about his previous business schemes."

"How would you make money fraudulently from houses that you had built?" Annie mused aloud.

"Well it comes down to a handful of possibilities," Gilbert suggested thoughtfully. "It might be that the land was bought cheaper than it should have been so therefore an extra profit could be made on the properties. Corners might have been cut in the construction of the properties or there could be something else going on that we simply aren't seeing."

"If the bungalows are also part of a scam, how do we determine that?"

Gilbert considered things for a moment or two.

"I have a friend in the planning office. I shall ask him a few questions, see if he can give me any information about the various planning permissions that have been granted to Mr Maguire and anything else to do with the sales of that particular patch of land."

"And what about Mr Mullins?" Annie asked.

"As you saw from that article I don't actually have an address for him. He disappeared not long after we published that piece, taking with him the rest of his fake coupons. He misled a lot of people in that particular incident, the police wanted to get hold of him, but they could never track him down."

"That doesn't help us at all, does it," Annie sighed. "Just when I thought we had something."

"You are far too easily defeated Annie," Gilbert said with a chortle. "This is all par for the course for doing something like this. We just need to dig deeper into the matter. One way or the other, we will figure this out."

Gilbert sounded confident, but Gilbert always tended to sound confident, or should she say cocky. Perhaps that was just the nature of being a journalist.

"I suppose it wouldn't hurt to look in a street directory to see if any Mr Mullins live around this area," Annie said after a moment. "He would be in the book if he owns a property around here."

"You would imagine so," Gilbert agreed. "Though I would've thought the police would have tracked him down already if it was that easy."

"In my experience, the police don't always think so laterally," Annie remarked. "I can see them not spending a great deal of time over this coupon scandal, considering it was not one of the biggest crimes going on in the area. They are always under pressure to investigate certain crimes and ignore others. A coupon scandal would be an easy one for them to overlook."

"I'm glad to see you have such faith in the police," Gilbert chuckled even harder. "Does Inspector Park-Coombs know how little you value his investigative abilities?"

"I am not suggesting that they are incapable of investigating something, my point is that in the scheme of things fake coupons that were sold to gullible housewives are not quite like things being stolen or people being killed. We both know the police have far too many crimes to solve and not enough time on their hands."

"If you say so," Gilbert was still amused. "Should I get the street directory out here and now so we can both look at it?"

"If you wouldn't mind," Annie said as politely as if she was talking to a bishop.

Gilbert went and fetched a battered street directory. It was the latest edition. He thumbed through it to the section marked M.

"There are three people with the name Mullins listed," he told Annie showing her the page. "I'll make a note of their names and visit them. Do you want to come with me?"

Annie almost said no, she fancied she had been out of the house for a good deal longer than she had meant to be that day, she had her chickens to think about and the dogs. She had asked one of the neighbours to pop in and make sure they were all right while she was out, knowing that she would be gone for quite a few hours and that Tommy would be busy, but she didn't like to think that she had just abandoned them all day.

She also had failed to do any cooking which was very unlike her. A part of her wanted to get home and go back to her usual routine, but it was immediately quashed down by another part of her that knew there was an injustice here that had to be resolved. Not just the one involving Tommy and Clara, she was also thinking of Miss Pendleton and all those poor ladies who had been scammed into buying books of coupons they couldn't use. It didn't take her long to make up her mind.

"I am going nowhere, Gilbert. I am with you until the bitter end."

Gilbert's grin grew broader. She wondered why everything amused him so much.

"Well then, best we get going, we have an awful lot of people to talk to."

With that he grabbed his hat up off the desk, in the process dislodging a pile of papers that spilled out across the floor. Annie looked aghast at the mess, but Gilbert didn't even seem to notice. Before she could say anything, he had caught hold of her elbow and was moving her towards the door.

"No time like the present Mrs Fitzgerald."

Annie suddenly worried about what she was getting herself into.

Chapter Ten

There were five names on the list that the tobacconist's wife had given to the police at the time of the robbery. Three of those names had been marked as deceased. The two remaining, living, individuals had once been delivery boys for the tobacco shop, and would have known about the secret safe.

The police had not actually taken the time to interview these two after they had focused on Joseph. His confession had pretty much ended their investigation. Clara didn't wish to say that this seemed slightly sloppy work, she could easily see how Inspector Park-Coombs would have considered the case closed as soon as Joseph admitted to the robbery. Why would he dig into the matter any further?

The police reports at least contained the addresses for the two individuals, even if the police had never visited them. Taking note of these addresses, Clara and Tommy headed off once again.

Both of them were beginning to feel quite cold after the long day traipsing around town and Clara found her thoughts constantly turning back to her snug home, warming herself before the fire and having an early supper with Captain O'Harris. Tommy was contemplating the fire in his own parlour and sitting before it with the dogs at his feet. He had made sure that Pip and Bramble had a good walk that morning before they started investigating so hopefully they would be quite settled for the rest of the day and wouldn't bother Annie too much. The dogs always tended to be a little restless when he was not at home.

They made their way to the first address and rapped on the door. The gentleman they were seeking was called Martin Lane. He had worked at the tobacco shop shortly before the war. Clara wondered what he would make of their questions.

The door was answered by a woman of around Clara's age, she was bouncing a young child on her hip. The child was grisly and was poking a wooden toy into its mouth while grumbling to itself. From its reddened cheeks and look of distraction Clara surmised the little one was teething and was having a bad time of it.

"Yes?" The woman asked them a tad sharply; she looked fraught, her hair, which she had carefully tied back that morning, was now falling loose and there were bags under her eyes. She was no doubt sleeping even worse than the child.

"We are looking for Martin Lane," Clara explained. "We hoped he might be at home. This is the correct address for him, I presume?"

"This is his home," the woman declared. "But he isn't here in the middle of the day, he's at work."

"And where does he work?" Tommy asked.

The woman nodded her head across the road and they both turned around to find themselves looking at another row of houses and beyond that a distant cemetery.

"He works over there. He's a gravedigger when he isn't acting as a pallbearer. If you want him, you best go have a look around the cemetery. He's always doing something around there."

With that the woman went back into her house and shut the door firmly in their faces. Clara did not take her rudeness to heart;

she surmised the woman was feeling a little bit overwhelmed by motherhood and had no time for two strangers asking random questions about her husband.

"Ready to go into a cemetery?" Clara glanced at her brother.

Tommy merely shrugged his shoulders. They headed across the road and through a gap in the houses, down a lane, towards the cemetery beyond. The cemetery had been built in the middle of the last century as a place to bury the dearly departed of the ever-expanding town. The regular churchyards were becoming overcrowded, and with many of those living around the area not being in regular attendance at a church (and thus seen by some as to not warrant taking a space in the churchyard which should have been kept for one of the faithful) a purpose-built cemetery was needed.

The graveyard was a large sprawling section of open ground which rippled up and down as it ran slowly uphill away from them. It was fenced in by dark black railings and tall gates which were currently open. There was a house built just inside the gate where the cemetery caretaker would reside. The lodge looked like a nineteenth century folly, but its presence made sure that there was always someone on site keeping an eye on the cemetery and the small chapel set within the grounds. As they were approaching, a horse drawn hearse was then leaving through the gates. They stepped out of the way to respectfully let it pass. Tommy took off his hat and pressed it to his chest while Clara politely dipped her head. The hearse was empty however, so they were paying their respects to empty air.

"Seems ever such a long time ago we were here for mother and father's funeral," Tommy remarked as they headed through the gates and along the path.

"I haven't been back since," Clara responded to him. "I suppose that is terrible. I made sure the headstone was all arranged of course, but I never come up here to tend the grave as you are supposed to. I just never felt I could. I don't think of them being in that grave you know? Their mortal remains might be, but I like to suppose that the rest of them went somewhere else."

"That sounds almost spiritual Clara," Tommy cocked his head in her direction. "And here was me thinking that you were quite the heathen."

"I don't know what I believe," Clara told him firmly. "But I am not so appalling as to suppose there might be nothing after death."

They followed the path that wound through the cemetery, at points it divided into different junctions taking them around the various sections of graves. They eventually spotted in the distance people stood around a newly dug grave. Those gathered around the graveside were paying their last respects to the deceased, while a short distance away two gravediggers stood watching while leaning on their shovels.

Clara could well imagine they were rather keen to be filling in the grave, their fingers numb with cold despite their gloves and their breath forming misty clouds before their mouths. The weather was on the turn again, the wind was getting up and the threat of rain was building in the air. The grave diggers would prefer to avoid backfilling the grave while it was raining down hard on them.

Clara wandered over in their direction, trying to be as discreet as possible so that the mourners would not be disturbed.

The two men watched her idly as she approached. The older of the pair had a thick moustache that masked his mouth and was wearing a weathered flat cap. He leaned on his spade as if it were the only thing holding him up. His younger companion was a reasonably good looking fellow though he was missing a front tooth which he revealed when he smiled at them in response to Clara's greeting.

"Sorry to disturb you when you are busy," Clara began. "I was hoping to speak to Martin Lane?"

The younger of the two workmen held out his hand to her. It was covered in the dirt of the graveyard but, since he had offered it, Clara didn't feel she could refuse shaking his hand. It was not all that often a man offered her a hand to shake, though she found the younger generation were better at doing this than the older.

"I'm Martin," the hand shaker explained. "How can I help you?"

"We wanted to ask you about the tobacco shop where you worked before the war," Tommy said, coming up beside his sister.

"Mr Greaves' old store?" Lane looked puzzled by the statement. "I haven't thought about that place in years."

"Were you aware that it was robbed last year?" Clara asked him.

"We read about that in the paper," it was the older man who answered her.

"That's right Pa, we did, didn't we?"

"You don't happen to know anything about the robbery?" Clara asked.

"Why would I?" Martin shrugged. "I haven't been back to that shop in years. I don't smoke, so no need to go there. "

"We were just trying to get our heads around the case," Clara explained to him. "The gentleman who was convicted of the crime has never protested his innocence, but his father is convinced that he is innocent and that he is protecting someone else. I don't suppose you remember where you were on the day the robbery took place?"

Clara quickly flipped open her notebook where she had made a note of the date of the crime and read it out to them.

"How would I remember where I was on that day last year?" Martin looked bemused by the suggestion.

"Hang on a minute, are you accusing my son of committing this crime?" The senior Mr Lane was becoming agitated by their questions.

"Not exactly," Clara said hastily. "We're just trying to figure out if Joseph Nunn, the man accused of the crime, might actually have an alibi. We are seeking out people who might have seen him around the time of the crime."

It was a complete fabrication, and a somewhat bumbling explanation, but the Lanes seemed to accept Clara's answer without questioning it too deeply.

"I don't know the fellow who was accused of the crime," Martin shook his head. "I remember thinking how awful it was for Mrs Greaves to be robbed like that. I felt really sorry for her. All the things she's gone through, losing her husband in the war, and trying to keep the shop going, the last thing she needed was something like that occurring."

"It has been a struggle for her then, has it?" Tommy asked.

"Isn't everything a struggle these days?" Martin replied. "It wouldn't be so bad if that son of hers actually helped from time to time, but he's always been something of a loafer."

"Mrs Greaves said her son is working on becoming an engineer," Clara said.

"Stuart is always working on *becoming* something," Martin snorted. "I remember when I worked at the shop he was always supposed to be learning one thing or another so he could make something of himself. For a time he was going to be a teacher, that was before the war of course. He went away to serve before I did, when he came back as far as I know he didn't do much of anything, certainly didn't resume his training to be a teacher."

At that point, the senior Mr Lane nudged his son and discreetly motioned towards the grave. The last mourner had departed, and it was time for them to get about their own work before the heavens opened on them and they were shovelling mud back into the grave.

"Sorry I can't help you," Martin told Clara. "I don't know the fellow who robbed the place, I am just very sorry that it happened."

Clara didn't detain them any longer, she didn't feel as though there was anything much to be gained from questioning them further. They had no evidence that Martin was the one behind the crime, and if he didn't know Joseph then why would the latter be protecting him by taking the blame on himself?

She walked away with Tommy just as the first spatters of rain began coming down. Knowing they were about to get drenched, they darted into the wide porch of the chapel to wait out the worst of the storm that was about to hurtle down.

"I don't think he's our robber," Clara said to her brother.

"No, there seems no reason to really suppose he would be involved. He has a steady job after all."

"That doesn't necessarily mean anything," Clara pointed out. "But my thinking is that he seems to have no connection to Joseph and if that's the case then there would be no reason for Joseph to take the blame and defend him. It seems to me that he is a dead end, so we shall try our last name on the list and hope for something to come of it."

They huddled in the porch as the rain tumbled down around them, watching it cascade off the roof in miniature waterfalls. They were stood there for some time waiting for the downpour to finish, and when they were done they both agreed to head back to Tommy's home and have a cup of tea and some lunch before they carried on.

Clara was still not sure what to make of the puzzle that was Joseph Nunn and his determination to take the blame for a crime he did not commit. Whatever the truth of this matter, she was going to find it out and reveal it to the world.

Chapter Eleven

Annie glanced at her watch again. The day was pushing along nicely, and here she was still out with Gilbert. She had not done her laundry for the day, nor had she done her weekly dusting. She had not refilled the coal scuttle or completed any of the dozens of tasks that she usually performed during the course of a week. In Annie's mind the house was about to go to rack and ruin without her firm hand at the tiller, all because she spent a few hours absent from it. She reminded herself for the umpteenth time that she was doing this for the benefit of Tommy and Clara. She had not gone on this adventure on a whim, and she was certainly not doing so because it could be considered fun. No, she was doing this for the benefit of her family and if that meant some sacrifices had to be made in regard to her housework, so be it.

She just hoped the dust didn't build up too much in her absence.

Gilbert had arranged the addresses for the three Mr Mullins in the directory in the most efficient order to visit them. He suggested they go to the farthest address first and work their way back to the *Gazette* office.

Annie agreed with Gilbert's logic, she had a similar method when going out to do her shopping. She always preferred to go to the shop that was furthest away and then work back towards the house than the other way around. It probably made no difference in terms of time or distance, but somehow it felt better to work from farthest to nearest. As if one was getting closer to success each time they moved a step closer to home.

Gilbert told Annie they would have to go on foot from now on. The car was only for long journeys where it would be inconvenient to use the bus. But he couldn't afford vast amounts of petrol for it, and he was quite prepared to walk when he needed to. Having shown her on the street directory map where the addresses were, Annie agreed that a combination of walking and short trips on the local bus would be the most convenient way of getting to each address. Annie typically walked everywhere and so she was not put out by this suggestion.

Despite the approach being sensible, Annie was slightly anxious when they first boarded the bus, wondering if any of her friends might notice her with the ungainly Gilbert McMillan. Fortunately, none of her neighbours or friends were on the bus. They were no doubt all at home sorting out meals or doing their housework. Annie found herself envying them and their quiet, ordinary, mundane little lives. She liked ordinary and mundane; it made her feel at peace.

Annie had no ambitions beyond being an excellent cook and housekeeper. She was not like Clara, who wanted to make something of herself in the world. Annie just wanted to be in the background quietly making sure that the world ticked over while the likes of Clara got on with being centre stage. It might not be ambitious, some women might even think she was somewhat pathetic for wishing to spend her days as a contented housewife, but Annie would argue that without people in the background doing all those mundane tasks that were needed to keep everything working, those people who wanted to be at the forefront of things couldn't be getting on with anything.

Meals didn't cook themselves after all.

Still, when needs must, Annie was prepared to go on an adventure.

They arrived at the furthest address a short time after boarding the bus. It was set in a little back street, in one of the older districts of the town. A person who took photographs for picture postcards might describe the houses as quaint – they would certainly look that way with a sepia tint over them in a photograph. But in the cold light of a chill, wintry day they looked rather run down and shabby. Despite the street having an air of neglect about it, it was obvious that some effort was made in keeping the homes comfortable. Annie observed that most of the front doorsteps of the houses had been scrubbed if not that morning, certainly the day before, and the windows were all clean and sparkling. She approved of these standards and felt that this was a street that housed a good quality of people, but perhaps who were slightly too poor to do running repairs to their homes.

Gilbert was glancing at a piece of paper in his hand then looking up at the houses, trying to pair up what he had written down with what he could see. After walking in one direction for a few paces, he stopped and turned around, walking back to Annie before finally deciding on a particular property. The source of his confusion was that most of the houses did not bear a number. This was an area where the postman knew everybody by name and house numbers were rarely required as the majority of the letters these people received were from family and close friends, who knew exactly where they lived. Gilbert finally decided he had found the right house and went through a narrow gate that was almost falling off its hinges. Just two paces along a broken path, he was at the front door and knocking on it.

Annie followed quietly behind Gilbert, looking around her and feeling uncomfortable. She found herself wondering how she had ever managed to walk up to the front door of Mr Maguire and accost him the other day, all she felt now was stomach churning nerves. She didn't like going to the homes of strangers, and she didn't like meeting people unannounced and uninvited.

There was no answer at the front door. Gilbert scratched his head under his hat, tilting it to one side as he considered their next move.

"It may be the wrong Mr Mullins," he said under his breath.

Annie wasn't sure if the comment was directed at her, or it was just him speaking his thoughts. At that moment, she noticed that a woman had come out of her house two doors down. The woman was attempting to look as though she was shaking out a rug in the garden, but Annie knew such tactics all too well. In a street like this, it was probably uncommon to see strangers and the lady was wondering who they were. She had picked up any old rug to shake outside to make it look as though she wasn't actually spying on them.

Annie made a snap decision and abandoned Gilbert to walk down the street to the woman shaking out her rug. The woman started to head back inside at the sight of her approach, uneasy that she had been spotted. Annie called out to her.

"We're trying to locate Mr Mullins; do you happen to know where he is?"

The woman paused with one foot on her doorstep.

"I do know where he is, but you won't have much luck speaking to him."

"Why is that?" Annie asked politely.

"Because he's been six feet under for the past two weeks," the woman explained bluntly and with no appearance of finding the topic unsettling. "I thought you might be some more of those debt collectors who have been coming around these last few days seeking him out."

Annie was perplexed by this statement.

"We have nothing to do with debt collection," she said, wondering if she looked like a lady who would be going around collecting debts.

For that matter, did women go around acting as debt collectors?

"We wanted to ask him a few questions about someone he might know. What happened to him?"

"We were told it was a heart attack," the woman explained, she had turned from the door now and was leaning against the brick wall that divided her small yard from the neighbours. "He always said he had something of a weak heart. Mind you, I don't suppose that argument he had with the fellow the night he died helped much. It was a real slanging match. All sorts of foul language could be heard coming from the house. I was about to ask my Arthur to go over there and have words, when suddenly we heard a door slamming and the gentleman visitor departed. About half an hour later we heard Mr Mullins calling for help out of an open window. He hadn't locked his front door, so we were able to burst in and found him lying on his bed, his hand clutched to his chest. We did try and send for a doctor, but he was done for."

If this was the Mr Mullins they were hoping to seek out and ask for answers about the activities of Mr Maguire they were quite clearly going to be disappointed.

"Why did you want to see him again?" The woman asked.

Annie almost said it didn't matter, then she stopped herself. She had an idea; it was the sort of thing Clara would do, and Clara always got the information she needed.

"I was told Mr Mullins sold useful books of grocery coupons," Annie said. "I was hoping to purchase a book."

"And who told you that?" The woman now stared at her with narrowed eyes.

"I have a friend who had purchased a book of these coupons. She showed them to me, and I thought they were a grand idea. Everything is so expensive these days, don't you find?"

"Well your friend is a fool," the woman fixed Annie with a stony gaze. "Those books of coupons are all a sham. I should know, Mr Mullins gave me a book after I helped him with some work around his house. At the time I thought to myself what a kindness it was, and then I tried to use them and was told they weren't valid. When I went and confronted him about it, he made some cock and bull story about there being a misunderstanding. You ask me, I think he was planning on being away from this street before I ever used the coupons so I would never be able to come back at him. He thought by giving that booklet to me it would prevent me from asking for any sort of favour in return for what we had done for him."

The woman shook her head sadly.

"Of course, it all fell flat for him, he was not meant to still be here. He told my Arthur that more than once. He was supposed to be coming into a lot of money."

"Any idea how he was supposed to be coming into that money?" Annie asked.

"Couldn't tell you, but he was the sort of fellow who was always up to some scheme or another. But now he is dead, and all his sins will finally be found out and laid before him. Do you believe in God?"

Annie nodded her head in the affirmative.

"Well, all I can say is Mr Mullins is now meeting his maker, and I bet it's a right old serious conversation they're having. You ask me, he's going to be heading down instead of up."

The woman emphasised this statement by pointing first down then up.

"Sorry you've come on a wasted journey but at least you won't be spending money on fake coupons," she added before she went back into her house and closed the door.

Annie headed back to Gilbert who was still trying to get someone to come to the door of the house. Annie admired his persistence, but she did think that sometimes you had to just accept a house was empty. Though, knowing Gilbert, he probably went to a lot of houses where people refused to answer the door. He was just turning around on the doorstep when he spotted Annie coming back down the road. He had failed to notice her absence.

"I'm pretty certain this was the right Mr Mullins," Annie told him. "I just spoke with a neighbour, and she confirmed that this gentleman was selling books of coupons, but we're two weeks too late. He suffered a heart attack and died."

Gilbert scratched at his hair again.

"Then the fellow is long gone and can't tell us anything in person, but that doesn't mean he can't still be of use to us."

Annie wondered what he was up to. She didn't have to wonder for long because Gilbert turned around, glanced at the front wall of the house, and then bent down to fumble under a flowerpot. He stood up again brandishing a key.

"Gilbert, you are not about to do what I think you are about to do, are you?"

Annie watched on in horror as Gilbert placed the spare key he had located into the lock of the front door and opened it.

"The man is dead Annie," Gilbert said over his shoulder. "If we want information we have to be bold."

"This is breaking and entering!" Annie hissed at him.

"It is not breaking and entering when you use the actual front door key," Gilbert told her bluntly. "Besides, this is just the sort of thing I do all the time."

Annie was acutely aware that this was also the sort of thing that

Clara did all the time. But it *wasn't* the sort of thing that Annie did. There was nothing she could say to deter Gilbert. He was already inside the house and wasn't waiting to see if she followed him. Glancing up and down the road to see if anybody else was watching them, Annie made another impulsive decision. Mr Mullins was dead; he didn't own this property and any possessions he had left within it would simply be discarded as soon as the landlord came to reclaim the house. It might even be the case that it had already been emptied. If they wanted any information this was perhaps the only chance they had.

Glancing back and forth one more time, Annie resolved herself. Hoping she wouldn't end up regretting her decision she stepped forward into the house. She was about to trespass on someone else's property, but she told herself it was all in the name of a good cause.

After all, Mr Mullins was a wrongdoer. If there was anything here that could link him to Maguire and help her cause then she had to find it, whatever the cost.

Chapter Twelve

Tommy was surprised to find his front door locked when he pushed on it. Frowning, he pulled his key out of his pocket and opened the door, only to be greeted by a boisterous Labrador who barrelled into him and nearly took him out. Pip bounced up on him and tried to lick his face as if he had been gone for a year or more.

In contrast, Bramble, a small and dainty black poodle, was more reserved in his affection and stood back and waited for the big blunderbuss that was Pip to get her enthusiasm out of the way before he too came forward and hopped up on his back feet at his master's legs. Tommy greeted the dogs affectionately, patting Pip's head, and rubbing Bramble under the chin just as he liked it. Then he looked up into the empty house. There was no sound of cutlery being moved, no pots and pans rattling, no smells of food cooking.

"Where is Annie?"

Clara came up behind him and glanced in through the front door, the first thing she noticed was that Annie's hat, coat, and scarf were missing.

"I would say that Annie is out on some sort of errand," Clara responded.

"It is unlike her to miss lunch," Tommy said still looking a bit troubled by her absence. "She always gets most agitated when *I* miss lunch."

"Then it must have been very urgent," Clara responded. "Maybe she left you a note to explain what she was doing."

They headed through into the kitchen with the dogs running around their feet. Clara immediately opened the kitchen door so they could bumble into the backyard. She took note the chickens had all been fed that morning and were clucking around contentedly in their run. The house seemed to be in fine order, just missing its usual caretaker. Tommy had been looking around the kitchen for a note left by Annie and had finally discovered it propped up against the kettle.

"She just says she had a few things to do and might be late home today," Tommy said after he had scanned the note. "She says she will certainly be back to make dinner and not to worry it's nothing important. She's added a little 'PS' at the bottom to tell us that there is bread and ham in the pantry if we want sandwiches."

"Annie is ever efficient," Clara said with a smile heading into the pantry to find the food that her sister-in-law had left out for them. She discovered a large, boiled ham sitting in the coldest corner of the pantry and a fresh loaf of bread. Bringing them both through to the kitchen table, she cut the meat and made-up sandwiches for them while Tommy paced back and forth looking worried.

"Annie has been acting odd lately," he said suddenly.

"Odd?" Clara asked him.

"Going out early, and not being at home as often as usual," Tommy said, trying to explain why he was feeling so concerned, but not quite sure how to put it into words.

The changes he had noticed in Annie were subtle, and not something it was easy to put a finger on, they were the sort of difference that only a person who lived with another for an extended time would notice.

"Perhaps Annie has a new hobby," Clara remarked. "Remember when she first got interested in keeping chickens. She was out at all manner of strange times visiting other people who kept chickens before she decided to bring that coop home."

"That's true," Tommy said. "But that was also a long time ago, before we were married. I wouldn't have expected her to tell me what she was up to back then, but these days I feel odd if she doesn't let me know where she's going. I start to worry about her a little."

"One thing I am very certain of, Annie is not likely to get herself into trouble," Clara said with a smile. "She isn't me, for a start. Annie is far too sensible to get caught up in any of the sorts of nonsense that I do. More than likely she is planning something. Maybe she has finally discovered someone who can teach her how to preserve peaches as she has always wanted to learn."

"She *has* been talking a lot about growing her own cucumbers this year," Tommy added, now tapping his lip as he considered the matter. "She said she'd read about it in a magazine and was determined to give it a go, but she thought she might speak to a few people first. Perhaps she is seeking out some advice and visiting people in the process."

"When it comes to the mysteries of Annie, the most likely thing is that she's on some culinary adventure, finding out new recipes or ways to do things," Clara concurred with him. "It's entirely possible she is on a mission to learn how to be the best cucumber grower in the county."

Tommy felt a fraction better after she had said this. He took a long deep breath in and then came over to eat his sandwich. He generously shared the corners with the two dogs who had hurried back inside to see what he was up to.

"What did you make of Martin Lane?" He asked his sister after a moment.

"I saw no reason to suppose he had suddenly decided to rob the shop where he used to work," Clara responded. "Admittedly, I don't suppose he makes a great deal of money as a gravedigger, and it is possible that he suddenly decided he needed some extra cash."

"They have a baby after all," Tommy remarked. "Thinking about the age of the child, his wife would have been pregnant at the time of the robbery. Maybe they needed a little extra money to help them through or maybe he wanted to put some away to look after her when she'd given birth?"

"That is all good speculation, but we have nothing to prove it. More to the point, why would Joseph protect Martin Lane? They were not even friends. No, there has to be some connection between the person who committed the robbery and Joseph, that's the only way this makes sense."

Tommy mulled this over as he ate some more of his sandwich.

"What if none of this makes sense?" He said at last.

He didn't just mean the case they were working on; he was also referring to the absence of Annie.

Having concluded their lunch they decided to take the dogs with them as they headed out again to locate the last name on the list they had acquired. This particular person did not live far away from them, and it would only take a short walk to reach their address, which would make it a good opportunity for the dogs to stretch their legs. Tommy was still uneasy that Annie was absent when they left the house. Clara tried to distract him as they walked along, she holding the lead of Bramble while he clung to the lead around Pip's neck. Pip pulled like a dray horse, always assuming they were heading somewhere good when they went out on a walk. Tommy had yet to master the art of getting her to walk to heel, mainly because he hadn't really tried. With a gagging, choking Labrador on the end of the lead he guided their way along the roads until they reached the final address on the list.

The property was the home of a gentleman by the name of Winston Keats. Tommy had been thinking about the name the whole time they were walking; something about it was ringing a bell.

"Keats," he said to himself aloud. "Do you know Clara, I could have sworn I served with a man called Keats. He was a private and he joined our regiment not long before I was wounded and sent home. For the life of me I can't remember whether his first name was Winston."

"If he was part of your old regiment then that would give us our connection to Joseph," Clara remarked as they reached the house.

It was a pleasant semi-detached property, built in the last decade or so, with a bay window to the right of the front door, and a well-established garden with a stone bird bath in the centre of the lawn. Clara knocked and waited a moment for a response; it wasn't long before an older woman answered the door. She was just as neat and well turned out as the house itself; she was wearing a fancy apron and appeared to have been cooking, though Annie would have commented that an apron with such an array of frills around the edge could hardly be practical for such an activity.

"Can I help you?"

"I apologise for disturbing you," Clara said. "I wondered if we could speak to Mr Winston Keats."

"You want to talk to Winnie?" The woman looked worried all of a sudden. "I am very sorry, but you won't find him here."

"Winnie Keats!" Tommy, stood just behind his sister, suddenly recalled the name. "Of course, I should have realised he went by Winnie in the trenches."

The woman on the doorstep now glanced over at him.

"You served with my son?"

"Captain Thomas Fitzgerald," Tommy introduced himself to the woman. "I'm afraid I only briefly knew your son before I was injured and sent back home an invalid."

"So many people came back broken from the war," Mrs Keats said quietly. "Winnie has never been the same since he came back."

"We wanted to talk to him about before the war," Clara said carefully. "And his connection with Joseph Nunn."

"Oh my, is Joseph all right?"

"He is doing as well as can be expected," Tommy explained. "I wasn't aware that Joseph was keeping in touch with Keats."

"Joseph has been very good to my son," Mrs Keats explained, "When he came back from the war he was a different man, we couldn't get any word out of him. He shut down completely, but Joseph has been trying to help him to come back to life. I don't know if he will ever be normal again, but if he could at least live a proper life that would be something."

Clara was intrigued that there was this connection between two men who had both worked at the same tobacconist shop, one before the war and one after.

"Where will we find your son?" She asked Mrs Keats. "We just want to ask him a few questions to help Joseph who has been placed in a very difficult situation."

"Is this to do with the robbery of the tobacconist's shop?" Mrs Keats asked tears forming in her eyes, "I feel dreadful about that business you know."

She fumbled in the pocket of her apron and pulled out her handkerchief, dabbing with it at her eyes.

"It never should have gone to court, we told Mrs Greaves we would pay the money back. But she was so determined to have someone blamed for the crime, and to see that person prosecuted. Nothing we attempted to do privately would please her."

"The way you're talking it sounds like you know a lot more about this robbery than the rest of us," Tommy said, stepping forward. "You knew that Joseph had stolen the money from Mrs Greaves?"

The woman glanced between them, then she shook her head.

"I really shouldn't say anymore."

"If there is more to say it ought to be said aloud," Clara hastily told her. "Joseph's father has asked us to prove that his son was innocent of the crime. He does not believe that Joseph was responsible for the robbery. I believe that Joseph is covering for someone, that he is doing so at great sacrifice to himself because he feels it is his duty. He has placed himself in a terrible position, and now they have rescinded his Victoria Cross."

"They did what?" Mrs Keats looked horrified at the news. "How could they do that? He was so brave the day he earned that. Do you know one of the men he saved in that act of heroism was my own son Winnie? He has been looking out for Winnie all these years like he was a baby brother to him. But he can't do this anymore."

Mrs Keats bit at her fingernail trying to come to a decision. After a moment, she took a deep breath and resolved herself.

"You must come in at once, I have a lot to discuss with you."

When asked if she minded the dogs coming in with them, Mrs Keats indicated she had no problem with their presence and then showed them into the house and through into her back sitting room. It was well appointed with soft, comfortable sofas and a handsome clock ticking away on the mantel. A gas fire had been installed in the hearth to replace the old coal one and it was quite obvious the family had money; so how could they be connected to the robbery?

Mrs Keats motioned for them to sit before she went to the mantlepiece and pulled out a cigarette from a box atop it. She offered the box to both Tommy and Clara, but they declined. Pip and Bramble gladly made themselves comfortable before the fire.

"I told myself I was giving up smoking when I had the children," Mrs Keats said. "And I was good for years and years, then the war came, and both my Archie and Winnie went off to serve. After that I just couldn't help myself, the cigarettes were a way of getting by and I've never kicked the habit since. My Archie didn't return from the war."

She paused and stared at the ticking clock.

"At least he left me well provided for, though I have to be careful and budget everything. The house is all paid for, thankfully, so I shall have a roof over my head until I die. The war really changed a lot of things. My Winnie was meant to go to university, to become an academic. He was going to study philosophy. We used to laugh and ask him how many uses were there for a philosopher these days, but he was determined. Then everything changed.

"Archie died and Winnie was terribly injured. They sent him home and he was never the same young man I knew before. He couldn't stay in the house, said it reminded him too much of the past and he ended up getting himself a small property. I don't know how he survives as he won't accept any money from me, and he is not in a fit condition to work. I heard rumours from other people that he had started to get himself into trouble. Drink is a problem for him, and he has fallen deeply into debt. I have tried to reach out to him but nothing I say or do seems to make a difference.

"One day last year I visited him, and he had all this money. He even gave some to his sister and me. The next thing I was reading about the tobacconist shop where he used to work being robbed. I put two and two together and realised what he must have done. My poor son, desperate and alone! The war broke him, you have to believe me, it is not his fault. He would never have survived prison. That would have been the end for him. I didn't know what to do. I ended up confiding my fears to Joseph, he was the only one I thought would understand. He told me not to worry and that he would sort everything out.

"The next thing I knew, Joseph Nunn had been arrested for robbing the tobacconist shop! He sacrificed himself for my son, yet again, just like he had done all those years ago back on the front. He is acting the hero once more, no matter what the cost to himself."

Chapter Thirteen

Annie had never gone exploring around another person's house before, certainly not a person who was dead. As she followed Gilbert into the house she became aware of how eerie the place seemed knowing that its former occupant was deceased. Gilbert moved behind her and carefully closed the front door.

"Don't want anybody seeing us."

Annie gave a shudder as she thought about what they were doing, what would Clara say if she knew? Well, knowing Clara she would probably be impressed. This was just the sort of thing that she did on a regular basis. Annie, on the other hand, felt self-conscious and was sure she was breaking any number of laws. She was probably even putting her immortal soul in peril.

At first she didn't move out of the hallway, just watching as Gilbert headed into the front sitting room and started fumbling around looking for anything that would give them a hint of the connection between Mullins and Maguire.

"Are you going to assist me, or are you just going to stand there?"

He called out after a moment.

Annie took a deep breath in; she had come this far, she might as well keep going. Telling herself that she was doing this all for the greater good, she headed to the back parlour and began her own search. There was a small writing desk in the room, it was rather old and looked like something that might have been used in a school in a previous life. There was a metal inkpot nestled in a hole at the top edge of the desk though it was currently empty.

Annie lifted the lid of the desk and looked inside. She was immediately greeted by several stakes of coupon books. She picked one up and flicked through the pages, finding an array of tempting offers. Everything from 2p off washing powder to half price joints of beef. The book looked professionally printed and seemed genuine. Annie unhappily wondered if *she* had been offered one of these books by someone who seemed respectable whether she would have been convinced to buy it? When she added up all the offers on the coupons she worked out the savings they would make a person would be substantial. Everybody was trying to save a penny or two these days. Suddenly she felt angry. Mr Mullins had been using people's fear of poverty against them. He had been targeting the poorest of people, stealing their last few pennies from them and leaving them worse off by persuading them he was helping them save money. All this just so he could make his own living.

Annie's discomfort at being in his house had suddenly evaporated. Mr Mullins was a crook just like his friend Mr Maguire, they both used other people and threw the blame for their misfortunes on others. Mullins had tried to scam people; Maguire was trying to get money out of Clara and Tommy for nothing.

Annie dumped the coupon book back in the desk and started to search around the parlour with renewed enthusiasm, looking for any information that could lead her to a better understanding of what Mr Mullins and Maguire were up to. The parlour proved fruitless for her search; apart from the coupons in the writing desk there was not much to be found though she did note that some papers had recently been burned in the fireplace. She used a poker to pull out the fragile remains but whatever they had once been they were too burnt to cinders to tell her anything. She just hoped they had not been important for making the connection between Mullins and Maguire.

Gilbert was still rummaging around in the front room; he didn't seem to be having any more luck than she was.

Annie headed into the kitchen and started to go through the dead man's cupboards. Annie believed that kitchens could tell you a lot about a person beyond what sort of tea they drank and whether they kept their dry goods in order. She swiftly discovered that no one had been in the kitchen for some time and a neglected mouldy loaf of bread was now developing into a greyish mound, almost possible to mistake for a cat, on the kitchen counter. She couldn't bear to look at it, instead taking it outside along with the bread board it was sitting on and dumping it into the nearest dustbin. Thankfully, the yard at the back had tall walls so that no one in the neighbouring houses should notice her or what she was doing, though whether they would even care that that she was disposing of mouldy bread was another matter. Back inside the kitchen she continued with her search.

Mr Mullins seemed to have been a man who lived frugally, his cupboards were largely empty even though there weren't that many of them. His pantry showed only the minimal of basic supplies. Annie surmised there was not a great deal of income coming in for Mr Mullins, yet he had told his neighbour that he was hoping to move away soon. He had been so certain he was going to be moving up in the world, in fact, that he had been prepared to give one of his neighbour's a booklet of fake coupons as a thank you, thinking that he would be long gone before they discovered his con.

It certainly told her everything she needed to know about the man; if there had been any doubt in her mind that he was a scoundrel and that he was liable to be friends with Mr Maguire then the evidence she had found would have removed it.

Having searched the cupboards and discovered nothing suspicious she was about to leave the kitchen when Annie had an idea. She might not be a detective, but she knew that people sometimes used their kitchens to store things other than just food. After all, she had a secret jar in her own kitchen which contained loose change she was keeping safe for a rainy day. Maybe Mr Mullins had done something similar?

Annie took another look around the cupboards and eventually found something that intrigued her. There was an old biscuit tin which, when she lifted it up, felt light as a feather. At first glance you would just assume it was empty, like so much else in the kitchen.

Now Annie decided to take a look inside – if it was empty, she had lost nothing, but if it was not...

Annie pried open the lid of the biscuit tin, which proved harder than she had expected, but was worth the effort for she revealed within an assortment of papers. She carefully emptied the contents on the kitchen counter and began to sort through them. The first paper was a deed for a land sale. When Annie read it thoroughly she realised it was the deed for the land that Mr Maguire had purchased for the bungalows, yet the document was in the possession of Mr Mullins. Did that mean that he had actually put the money forward for the purchase of the land?

Just beneath that document was a letter. It had been formally typed up by a land surveyor. It indicated that the land that had recently been purchased for a nominal sum was of no use for building. The surveyor explained that the sandy soil of the plot would mean subsidence would be a big issue for anything being built on top. There were other concerns including drainage and the proximity to the sea. The surveyor had made it very plain that it was unlikely any house built on the site would last more than a year or two before significant problems would develop. Even with substantial (and expensive foundations) building a house on that land was a fool's errand.

Suddenly things began to fall into place in Annie's mind. Here was a cheap plot of land that Maguire and Mullins had bought between them. The land was of no use to anyone because it couldn't be built on, at least it couldn't be built on by anyone who was a legitimate businessman and cared about the buyers. But if you were prepared to bend the rules and ignore the surveyors concerns then nothing was impossible. Considering how much Maguire was asking for the properties, he would have made a small fortune for a very minor investment.

With the land purchased, the next stage was for Maguire to acquire planning permission.

The council read Mr Maguire's planning application in November of 1923 and the planning committee had been split on whether to grant permission or not. Though they did not take into account the surveyor's report, which was outside the scope of their debate – it did not matter to them whether houses build on the cliffs were going to fall down sooner rather than later – they were concerned about the impact new houses would have on the views to the sea for the neighbouring homes.

There had also been two objections from the general public to the planning proposal.

The person who owned the land adjacent to that which was going to be used for the bungalows had made a protest about access to the houses and the fact that the land was meant to be left as common ground for grazing. There was an old and ancient bylaw that meant the clifftop meadows should be available for all those in the area to graze their cattle on. Though no one actually used it for that purpose anymore, the bylaws still stood and should have been upheld.

The second objection came from the person (unnamed in the letter) who had originally sold the land to Maguire.

The objections had been considered and dismissed; the split had been decided by one final vote in favour of Mr Maguire's proposal.

At first Annie was surprised that a bylaw had been so easily overlooked but then she noticed one final piece of paper at the bottom of the tin. Annie pulled it out and discovered it was a letter from the planning officer who was in charge of the proposal. He had written to Mullins, observing that though the bylaw was a concern, if he was given the right compensation he would make sure the problems went away.

Quite plainly, he was prepared to take a bribe to ignore the local bylaw and push through the planning permission.

Here it all was in black and white; they had bought the land cheap because it was supposed to be useless. They had then bribed a planning officer so that they could get permission to build houses and ignore a local ancient bylaw. Finally they had ignored the surveyor who had told them that any houses built on the land would suffer from subsidence within a year unless built with substantial foundations, and even then it was likely they wouldn't last a decade.

Maguire and Mullins were going to make a small fortune out of the people who bought the properties thinking they were going to get a good deal. No doubt there would be other things they had cut corners on when they built the houses, but those issues would only be found out months later after Maguire and Mullins had vanished and could no longer be held culpable.

So many pieces of the puzzle were slowly falling into place. No wonder Maguire was desperate to get the bungalows sold sooner rather than later – he could not afford to wait. If he left it too long the houses would simply start to disintegrate, and his ploy would be revealed.

"Gilbert you need to come see this," Annie called through the house.

Gilbert hastened towards her. It was plain he had found nothing through his efforts to search the front room thoroughly, though he had made himself red in the face. Annie showed him the first piece of paper, as he read through it, his eyes lit up.

"My, my, I was not anticipating that he was going to be *this* nefarious."

Annie showed him the next letter and finally the one about the bribe.

"This is very serious," Annie said quietly after Gilbert had read the documents twice.

"It is dreadful," Gilbert nodded his head. "It reveals that Maguire is not just deceiving people, but he is prepared to bribe officials to get what he wants."

"What do we do now?" Annie asked him.

Gilbert paused.

"You asked me to find information that you could use as leverage against Maguire. This is it, but this goes far deeper. You could use it to blackmail Maguire into giving up the defamation case and issuing an apology, or *we* could take it further. We could take it to the police and show them what has happened here. Prove to them that Maguire is a crook and see him arrested for fraud."

Annie wasn't sure; she glanced at the documents again.

"Aside from the planning permission and the fact that they bribed an official, is there any evidence here of Maguire doing anything wrong?"

Gilbert sighed as he looked at the documents.

"Well there's nothing illegal in purchasing land cheaply and there is nothing actually illegal in building a property on that land even though a surveyor has said it won't last very long. That's just foolishness. There is certain legislation in place to prevent shoddy building work, but that would have to be proved in the first instance. The only real proof we have of wrongdoing is this letter about the planning officer, however, it is addressed to Mr Mullins."

"And that means that it only refers to Mr Mullins," Annie sighed to herself. "We can't use that against Mr Maguire. He would just deny all knowledge and say that Mullins bribed the man without his knowledge."

"Precisely, so taking it to the police is probably not going to help us."

"But I don't like blackmail," Annie looked despondent.

Just when she thought they were getting somewhere she felt as though they had been given another setback. Here was evidence that something amiss was going on but it wasn't anything they could use legally, and her only option left seemed to be to accuse Maguire and see if he would back down from the defamation case.

"Do you suppose it was Mr Maguire who was here the night that Mullins died?" Annie asked. "The man he was arguing with."

"I would imagine so, he was probably telling him that there was no money coming because of everything going wrong," Gilbert shook his head. "But what does that matter?"

Annie frowned at the papers, her mind going over and over again what they should do.

"We have to find more," she said at last. "More evidence that Maguire is up to no good. I don't want to use blackmail against him, I want to do this properly. We need to prove he's a con artist and we need to find out more about this bribery. Will you help me?"

Gilbert grinned at her.

"In for a penny in for a pound, as they say."

Chapter Fourteen

Mrs Keats was deeply distressed by her confession. She leaned back against the mantel of the fireplace and placed her head in her hands. Clara rose from her chair and placed a comforting hand on her shoulder.

"You just wanted to protect your son," Clara told her gently.

"Joseph said we had to protect him," Mrs Keats explained. "He told me I mustn't say a word and that he was going to take the blame. I didn't want him to, but he refused to change his mind. He said it was his duty. I don't understand how a man could feel like that for another. How he could sacrifice his own life for my son."

"It's a difficult thing to explain," Tommy said quietly from the sofa, lost in his own thoughts as he considered the matter. "After being in the trenches though, you understand it. Something changes you out there and you are almost compelled to sacrifice yourself for others. After all, that's how Joseph earned his VC, by being prepared to risk his life for his comrades. That mentality doesn't cease once you get back from the front. You still feel responsible for the men who are under your command. More to the point, you feel a tad guilty about what they are suffering now and which you cannot change. People call it misplaced guilt, but when you have been instructed to look after those men, and then you cannot when you're back in civilian life, you feel this burden upon you."

Mrs Keats lifted her head and looked at Tommy. Her eyes were filled with genuine sympathy.

"You sound a lot like Joseph. I suppose I shall never really understand what that is like. I am truly grateful for what you, and all the others who served, did for us during the war. Protecting us, giving your lives for our freedom, I can never repay any of you. I just look at my son and how broken he is, and I feel this anger burning within me. The trouble is I don't know who to direct that anger at. At the Germans who started it all? Or at our own government who failed our young men? They promised the war would end swiftly, instead great horrors were inflicted upon the young. Now my son is home, and no one cares about what he went through or his ongoing suffering. Yes, maybe that is what makes me the angriest. That no one cares *now*. He gave his youth to the war, to save our country and when *he* needs saving no one gives a damn."

Mrs Keats pulled a handkerchief out of her pocket even though she was not actually crying. She clutched it tight in her fists, balling it up and squeezing it hard.

"You are quite right," Tommy told her. "Our government should be ashamed of how they are failing their servicemen. They were keen enough to send us all to war, but what do they do to help us now the war is over? I think a lot of people are disillusioned by everything that has occurred since 1918."

"Mrs Keats, we really need to talk to your son," Clara interjected softly. "We need to know what really happened at the tobacconist's shop."

"I know you need the truth," Mrs Keats said. "But I cannot see my son go to prison. He truly wouldn't survive the ordeal. Hasn't he already suffered enough?"

"But what about Joseph? His name has been sullied. His honour questioned. Doesn't he deserve some justice as well?"

"Of course he does," Mrs Keats wrapped the handkerchief around her fingers tightly. "That's why I told you in the first place what I suspected. But to take this further would mean involving the police. To exonerate Joseph would mean proving my son guilty and I can't allow that to happen, you do understand?"

Tommy rose from the sofa and came and stood before her, he met her eyes with his own deep brown ones and held her stare.

"Mrs Keats, as an ex-serviceman myself, I can safely say that your son would not want someone to take the blame for his actions. It will shame him more to know that his superior officer was denied his VC and dishonoured because he was trying to protect him from his own crimes. We should speak to him and hear what he has to say, the truth of it all. A man has to face the consequences of his actions, there is no getting away from that."

Mrs Keats shook her head.

"I just want to protect him."

"He is a grown man," Tommy continued. "He has made his choices. Perhaps, by protecting him in this way, you are preventing him from facing the truth, from actually healing himself. If he has done this once and got away with the crime, what is to stop him doing it again when there is no one to take the blame for him?"

Mrs Keats considered this for a moment. She continued winding the handkerchief around her hand over and over, flipping it around and pulling it through her fingers in a frantic gesture as she tried to consider the matter rationally.

"Do you really think he might do something like this again?"

"It is entirely feasible, once a man has done something like this once the odds of him doing it again are much greater," Tommy explained to her. "Unless, that is, they have suffered a consequence for it, then they might reconsider. At the very least we must speak to him."

Mrs Keats dropped her head and finally stopped playing with the handkerchief. She had listened long and hard and she had come to the conclusion that Tommy was right. Her son needed help, and he wouldn't get that help unless he faced up to what he was doing. By protecting him, perhaps all she was doing was helping him to stay in his quagmire of despair and hopelessness.

"I will take you to my son," she agreed at last. "You ought to know that he has never made mention of this robbery to any of us. It is as if it never happened. I almost wonder if he even remembers doing it."

"Well we shall see what he says when he talks to us," Tommy smiled at her. "Don't forget we're old chums, from the trenches, he should recognise me."

"That is something at least," Mrs Keats nodded her head. "I just need to get my coat and hat."

Mrs Keats departed from the sitting room, and they went out into the hall to wait for her. A short time later she returned dressed for the weather outside. It looked as though she might have been crying while she was out of sight. Clara made no mention of her red eyes; if the woman had chosen to cry privately she clearly did not want them making a fuss about it.

They headed out of the house, and it proved only a short walk from Mrs Keats home to where Winston rented a room. Mrs Keats explained how Winnie had never adjusted to how life was now compared to what it had been like before. He kept himself isolated and away from the world, taking odd jobs to make ends meet. She was lucky if she saw him once a week on a Sunday, though she tried to stay in touch with him as much as possible.

Having built a picture of her son for them she took them to a respectable looking terraced house with a narrow bay window at the front and a flower box attached to the windowsill. The box was currently devoid of flowers, but someone had recently tossed a handful of bird seed into it and the little sparrows were dancing around on the surface picking up the grains.

Mrs Keats knocked on the front door and a moment later a gentleman answered it.

"Mr O'Connor," Mrs Keats nodded to the man. "I have come to see my son."

Mr O'Connor was an older gentleman with a balding head and a large moustache, he said very little as he allowed Mrs Keats to enter followed by Clara and Tommy. Mumbling something about Winston being upstairs in his room and motioning a hand to the staircase in the hall, the gentleman then returned to a back parlour and ignored his visitors.

He paid no heed to the dogs and had already vanished before Tommy could ask if it was acceptable to bring them inside. He decided to take a chance as he did not intend to leave the animals outside alone.

Mrs Keats said nothing as she headed up the staircase; she knew where she was going, though her footsteps seemed to become heavier with each stride up the stairs. They came to a landing with three doors along it and Mrs Keats walked to the door furthest away from them, knocking upon it with only a hint of hesitation. Clara realised that this door would lead into a room that ran across the front of the house and would have a view down over the street below. It had probably been the master bedroom prior to the rooms being rented out.

There was a sound of movement within the room, but no one immediately came to answer the door. Mrs Keats gave an apologetic smile to Clara and then knocked again. Once more there was noise from within but no answer to the summons.

"Winnie, it's your mother."

Mrs Keats shuffled her feet and smiled nervously, clearly agitated, and embarrassed by the lack of response from her son.

She was about to knock again when someone moved towards the door, they heard footsteps heading towards them, and then the door opened a fraction.

"It is not Sunday," a husky male voice said from within.

"No, it is not. But I do need to speak to you Winnie, I have two people here to see you."

At the statement that he had visitors Winnie immediately slammed shut the door in his mother's face.

"I don't see visitors," he declared loudly.

Mrs Keats looked fraught, she glanced at Clara in despair not knowing what to do next. Tommy moved past his sister and came to stand beside the woman.

"Let me," he said before he lifted his fist and knocked on the door. "Private Keats, this is Captain Fitzgerald, you remember me don't you? I've come to check up on you. It's been too long hasn't it?"

From inside the room they heard a quiet voice.

"Captain Fitzgerald? I thought you were dead."

"Nope, not dead, I just never made it back to the front after I was shot in the leg. I was invalided out and confined to a wheelchair for quite some time, but as you can see I'm doing much better now. I'm trying to catch up with all my former comrades and find out how they're doing. I recently came across Captain Nunn. You remember him of course, don't you Winnie?"

Tommy threw in the nickname to try and encourage Winston to talk to them and to remind him of their shared history. It was a risk; Winnie might find being reminded of the war too much and sink into despair, on the other hand he might be inclined to remember the friendship he had once known from Tommy and Joseph while they were in the trenches.

There was silence from behind the door. Mrs Keats began to look increasingly anxious, and the handkerchief was back out of her pocket and being wound through her fingers again. The agitated gesture was getting a little bit on Clara's nerves.

"Private Keats I expect you to open this door for me," Tommy tried again, aiming for an authoritarian approach this time.

He was just thinking it hadn't worked and they might have to try returning on another day, when he heard someone come to the door and the handle turn. Private Winston Keats stood on the threshold.

He was a dishevelled looking young man a handful of years younger than Tommy; he had barely met the minimum age to make it into the war. Now he stood in his pyjamas before them, the striped clothing stained with what might have been tea or other substances and the buttons mismatched. He looked as though he had thrown on the clothes and taken no care in dressing himself. He was unshaved and his hair had not been combed in some time. It was a light blonde colour and fluttered over his face in loose greasy tendrils.

But it was Winnie's eyes that disturbed Tommy the most. He had seen that look in men's eyes before, but never outside of the front. It was a look of perpetual terror, as if the horrors of the war were still continuing inside his head. There was something glazed and distant about those eyes, as if Winnie had seen things he would never forget, and which tormented him to this day. In that instant, Tommy knew Winston Keats needed all the help he could give him, and that before this was all over, he was going to have a chat with Captain O'Harris about whether he would accept a day visitor to his home.

O'Harris' convalescence home for ex-servicemen was not about helping them recover from physical injury, but from mental injury and if anyone knew how to deal with a man who was clearly in the depths of shell shock than it had to be O'Harris and his team. Tommy hadn't seen a case like Winnie's in a long time. The man had been keeping himself so hidden away that no one knew just how terrible things had become for him.

It was quite obvious that he was still trapped in the mindset of fear and survival that had come over them all while they were in the trenches.

For Winston Keats, the war was still going on.

At first, no one seemed able to speak, then Pip broke the silence by going towards Winston and pushing her large head into his hand. He stroked her absent-mindedly and the faintest glimmer of a smile crept onto his lips. Then he focused on Tommy.

"Captain Fitzgerald," Keats said looking up with a slight hint of awe on his face at Tommy. "I'm sorry, I really thought you were dead when you vanished on the battleground that day. The machine guns were hellish on that march, so many men went down and never got up again."

"I was shot, like so many, and for a time, I thought I was a goner," Tommy explained to him. "Truthfully, when I was lying wounded and in agony in No Man's Land, I was almost inclined to be dead. But as you can see I survived one way or the other. Will you let me in so we can talk?"

Winston stepped back from the door which was as much of an invitation as they were going to get. They entered a room that, though slightly untidy around the edges, was still clean. Winston might not be doing much to look after his own appearance, but it seemed he still remembered some things from his days in the army. His bed was neatly made-up, and all his belongings were carefully arranged in an orderly fashion.

Winston looked uneasily around him, trying to think of somewhere he could suggest they sit; there was only one chair in the room.

The space reminded Clara a great deal of the room Joseph Nunn was living in, and she surmised that Joseph had recognised a great deal of himself in Winston. Perhaps that was why he had been so keen to help Winnie. He might not be able to sort his own life out, but maybe he could help the man who reminded him so much of himself?

"We want to talk to you about something," Tommy began. "It won't be an easy conversation, are you up for it?"

Winston looked uneasy.

"D... don't know, Sir.

"Well, we'll just go for it and see how we get along, shall we?" Tommy was using the bright and optimistic voice he had used so often when he was commanding men to do terrible things.

He had hoped to never have to use that voice again – the one that commanded men to go over the top and get shot to pieces.

"We want to talk to you about the robbery at the tobacco shop."

"The what?" Keats asked, confused.

"The robbery at the tobacco shop last year," Tommy persisted. "You robbed the shop, didn't you?"

Winston Keats' face fell as he looked appalled at this statement.

"What are you saying?" He demanded of them, glancing now at his mother. "Are you accusing me of being a criminal?"

Chapter Fifteen

Winston Keats was clearly angered by the suggestion that he had committed a crime. This was an unexpected response from him, even taking his mother by surprise.

"Why would you even suggest such a thing?" He demanded of them all.

Tommy was lost for words, he glanced at Keats' mother. She gulped and then resolved herself to tell the truth.

"Well... you see... it was like this," she began hedging. "The tobacco shop where you once worked as a delivery boy was robbed last year, around the same time you suddenly came into a bit of money. I found myself assuming..."

Mrs Keats didn't finish that sentence; it was all too obvious what she had intended to say, and she was now feeling deeply uncomfortable.

Winnie was scowling at them all.

"I have never robbed a shop, and I never intend to," he said firmly. "I am many things, but I am not a criminal."

He had clutched his hands into fists and looked fearsome. Tommy fully believed every word he said.

"It seems there has been a grave misunderstanding Winnie,"

Tommy spoke. "Not only did your mother believe you had committed this robbery, but your friend Joseph Nunn believed it too. He was so convinced that he took the blame for the act himself and ended up serving time in prison."

Winnie looked astonished by this statement. The colour slowly drained from his face and then a moment later he had to sit down hastily on his bed, the shock of the unexpected revelation overcoming him.

"Why would he do something like that?" He said.

"Joseph wanted to protect you," his mother spoke. "I wanted to protect you."

"You had nothing to protect me from," Keats shook his head. "I don't read the newspapers; they are too full of doom and gloom. I had no idea any of this had occurred."

"Did you not wonder where Joseph was for the few months when he was in prison," Clara asked.

Keats shook his head.

"You have to appreciate, I am so isolated here, and time drifts into one. I almost fancied that Joseph was finally finished with me. That he was at last sick and tired of my failings. Everyone ends up that way in the end when it comes to me. No one wants to know the young man who can barely leave his room."

"If this is all true Winnie, then where did that money come from?" His mother now demanded.

Winnie glanced in her direction, clearly confused.

"Money?"

"You suddenly had a lot of money. You even gave some to your sister."

"I didn't steal that money," Winnie said angrily, thinking back several months to a time when he had suddenly found himself flush with cash. "I will admit the money was curious, but it wasn't anything to do with a robbery."

"Then how did you come to have it?" Mrs Keats insisted.

"It was sent to me," Winnie said, looking at her innocently. "It was in an envelope sealed up with my name on it. It was pushed through the front door, and Mr O'Connor brought it up to my room and delivered it to me by hand. When I opened it, there was all this cash inside. There was nothing to say who it had come from."

"You must have wondered why that money had suddenly been sent to you?" Clara said to him.

"I did, but I supposed it was a gift from someone. At any rate, no one mentioned anything about it and as it was addressed to me I decided it was sent by someone wanting to show me some charity without revealing themselves. In truth, I can always do with extra money."

"You must see how this appeared to your mother and Joseph. You suddenly had an envelope full of cash right at the time a shop was robbed of a significant amount of money," Tommy tried to impress upon Keats how his mother and friend had ended up coming to the assumption they had made.

"I can see your point," Winnie admitted. "But I still insist that I am innocent. I was nowhere near the tobacco shop at the time of the robbery. I haven't been near that place, or in the street it resides in, in years. Other than this room, the only place I tend to go to is the pub just around the corner."

"But if this is correct," Clara spoke, "then Joseph Nunn took the blame for a crime that you didn't commit, and the real culprit has never been discovered."

Mrs Keats looked confused, still unable to fully believe that her son was innocent. She had so completely convinced herself of his guilt, that it seemed impossible now to believe him blameless.

"I don't suppose you have the envelope that the money came in, do you?" Clara asked Keats.

Winnie considered this for a moment, then he rose up and headed over to a small table in the corner of the room which was piled with books and papers. He rummaged around for a while before producing a scrap of paper. It proved to be the envelope which he had re-used to write out a series of calculations concerning his weekly outgoings. He gave it to Clara.

The envelope was tatty around the corners, and much creased but it was still possible to see the message printed on the back which clearly said that it was to be hand delivered to Private Winston Keats. Clara frowned; who had sent this money to Winston and for what purpose?

"How much money was in the envelope?" Clara asked him.

Winston considered the question for a moment, scratching at his head again.

"I think, there was about £15 inside," he said.

That was a significant sum; Tommy wondered how much had been stolen from the tobacco shop.

"I think we need to speak to Joseph Nunn again," He remarked. "We have to figure out where this money came from and who sent it to Winston. "

"Do you think it came from the robbery?" Winston now asked, his eyes had lit up and he no longer looked so dazed, as if he was finally taking notice of his surroundings.

"It is hard to say but it seems a very odd coincidence if it was not," Clara remarked. "It is possible that whoever stole the money was concerned that the police might come looking for them and decided to shift the blame onto someone who would be very easy to suspect of the crime."

"Someone was trying to put the blame for this crime on my son?" Mrs Keats asked.

"That seems a very strong possibility," Clara replied. "Whatever happened we need to find out where that money came from and who suddenly decided to give it to your son."

Winston could offer them no further information on the envelope, he could only tell them where he had spent the money. In the main, he had used it to pay off debts, some of which had been accrued as result of gambling. He admitted to his mother that he had been in a bad place at the time he had laid the bets – or, rather, a worse place than usual – and that he had learned his lesson and wouldn't be gambling again in the future. Whether she believed him or not, she did not rebuke him for the matter in front of Tommy and Clara. She was more interested in discovering who had attempted to frame him for the robbery and, inadvertently, set Joseph Nunn to prison.

Having gained all they could from Winston, Tommy and Clara made their excuses to leave and left him in peace. His mother came with them, looking troubled by everything she had just learned. She had believed her son capable of a crime without ever asking him about it. She was concerned what that might say about her as a mother.

"How could I believe he had committed such a crime?" Mrs Keats said as they were walking her home. "I thought my son a criminal with no real proof. Have I come to think so little of him I considered him capable of robbing a shop? I never would have believed such a thing before he came back from the war."

"The evidence you had was very plausible," Clara tried to console her. "It was not an unreasonable assumption. It is unfortunate that you came to that conclusion, but the situation at the time seemed to suggest there was only one possibility. I dare say, under the circumstances, it was an easy mistake to make."

Mrs Keats did not look convinced, but she accepted Clara's attempt to assuage her guilt.

"If you two had not come along I would have gone to my grave assuming my son was capable of robbing a shop. I have done him a great disservice."

"Try not to feel too bad about it," Tommy spoke. "If you would allow me, I would like to see if I can get some help for your son."

"Help?" Mrs Keats looked at him in surprise.

"We know someone who can help ex-servicemen who are suffering from what is called shell shock. Seeing Winnie just now I am convinced that is what is wrong with him. I have been there myself, Mrs Keats, I know what a dark and lonely place it is. But with the right treatment it can be made so much better. If you would allow me to find someone to assist him then perhaps we can bring your son back to you and give him back the life he deserves."

Mrs Keats did not know how to respond to this statement; she had thought for so long that her son was beyond all hope. The possibility he could be helped filled her with a perilous sense of hopeful joy, that rapidly faded into trepidation.

"Are you suggesting private treatment? That costs a great deal of money."

Sadness entered her tone.

"No, it should not cost much, if anything," Tommy promised her. "Let me just look into it, if you wouldn't mind?"

Mrs Keats considered for a while longer than agreed that Tommy could see about getting help for her son.

"We have tried various things over the years, even had the local vicar out who said he was going to perform an exorcism on my son as he was battling demons. I didn't really approve of such a superstitious thing and decided against it."

"In a way, the vicar was correct," Tommy said. "Your son is battling demons, but not the sort that rise from Hell. His demons are the metaphorical ones that are born and grown inside us. Give me a chance to help him, Mrs Keats, I swear I will do my very best."

"You are very kind," Mrs Keats said, hardly daring to hope that Tommy could fix her son. "Just like Joseph, who came along and said he would help Winnie and did. I do not know what my son, or I, have done to deserve such kindness in our lives from relative strangers but I very much appreciate it."

"People should not have to do anything to deserve kindness," Clara smiled at her softly. "Your son fought bravely in a war for all of us and he deserves better than what he is receiving right now."

Mrs Keats was touched, and the tears threatened to return. Before she could shed them in public, she wished them goodbye and headed into her house.

"I hope O'Harris won't be angry with me for offering his help for free," Tommy said once she was gone, looking slightly abashed as they walked away.

"You know O'Harris will help anybody who needs it," Clara smiled at him.

"If only I had known about Winnie Keats sooner," Tommy shook his head. "I am furious at how long he has been suffering like this with nothing being done for him. The shame of it all that he has been left in such a state! We all bear the burden of that responsibility."

"You did not know about his situation," Clara told her brother, trying to shake him out of his guilt. "You can't be held responsible for everybody who came back from the war."

"No, just the ones who I served with, who I commanded, and who I should be keeping an eye on even now."

"You take far too much responsibility onto yourself," Clara slipped her arm through her brother's. "Not everything falls down upon your shoulders alone, you know?"

"Come on Clara, you know how it is. I feel responsible for the men I was in charge of, just like you feel responsible for the people who you take on cases for."

Clara could not deny that was true.

"We will do our best to make this right," she promised her brother. "For now, we are a step further forward. We know that Joseph Nunn took responsibility for a crime he thought had been committed by an old friend, someone he wanted to protect. We also know that Winston Keats denies having any involvement in that crime, and the presence of the envelope which he said contained money seems to confirm his innocence."

"I suppose he could still be lying, of course," Tommy said, just to remind himself that nothing was ever as clear cut as it seemed. "But I really believed him when he insisted he was innocent."

"Keats looked very distressed about being accused of the crime. I want to believe him."

"Surely being a private detective is not about what you *want* to believe, but believing in what is actually true?" Tommy teased his sister.

"You have a point, but in this instance I'm going to trust my instinct. I feel that Keats is telling the truth, which means that someone else robbed that tobacco shop, and then they planted evidence on Keats hoping the blame would be deferred onto him."

"And they were so successful in their ploy they had Winnie's own mother believing he as a criminal. We need to find this person," Tommy said firmly. "First things first, we should go back and speak to Joseph Nunn. Find out what he can tell us about this. Maybe something was mentioned to him that will help shine a light on who could be the real culprit."

"First things first," Clara turned the phrase back to him, "let's go home and see if Annie has returned. The dogs have been out all afternoon and need their supper."

Pip who seemed to have a knack for knowing when food was being discussed suddenly glanced up in Clara's direction and wagged her tail vigorously. The dogs had been very well behaved, causing no bother during the interviews.

"You're right, we also need to find out if Annie has returned home yet," a troubled look crossed Tommy's face. "She is such a worry you know."

Clara laughed out loud.

"That is not a statement I ever thought I would hear you say about Annie!"

Chapter Sixteen

Annie had returned home by the time they arrived back at the house. When asked by Tommy about where she had been she made a vague reply about being busy on various errands, and that she had arranged for a neighbour to check on the dogs if no one had returned home by lunchtime.

Nothing more would she say on the subject, and she diverted the conversation by insisting Clara have a cup of tea and a slice of cake before she headed back to her own home. Clara suspected Annie was keeping secrets, but decided it was none of her business. She trusted her sister-in-law and knew Annie would tell her what she was up to when she felt ready.

Nothing more occurred that evening, and it was not until the following day that they once again set out on their investigation. Clara had updated O'Harris about what they were doing and the unfortunate business with Winston Keats over breakfast. O'Harris promised there was a space for him at the home if he needed it, and that he would be given the help he deserved, if he was prepared to allow them to assist him. That was often the greatest hurdle O'Harris, and his team of doctors, faced – persuading a man to come to the home and talk about himself. So many people thought that problems of the mind were a weakness, something to be ashamed of, which made it hard to talk to them. Clara could only hope that Winston would be willing to embrace the help he was offered.

After meeting up with Tommy, they set off to revisit Joseph Nunn and tell him about Winston's innocence in the robbery.

They found Joseph in his rooms. He was going through the newspaper, trying to find another job, one where his employer either did not know or did not care that his name had been splashed about in the newspapers when he was found guilty of robbing the previous place he had worked.

So far, things were not looking promising.

Joseph was looking even more haggard than the day before when he allowed them into his rooms. There were deep shadows under his eyes, as if he had not slept, and he had not shaved that morning. Tommy wondered just how well he was eating; he looked half starved.

Was he in such a bad place that he could not even afford food?

"What are you both doing back here?" Joseph asked them as soon as they were in his rooms. "I thought I told you everything you wanted to know when we last spoke."

"You didn't tell us everything," Clara corrected him as delicately as she could. "You didn't tell us the real reason you failed to protest your innocence when you were accused of robbing the tobacco shop. We know you were protecting Winston Keats."

Joseph tried to look surprised at the name, then turned away from them quickly in an attempt to hide his emotions.

"We know the whole story, old boy, "Tommy elaborated. "We have been to see Mrs Keats and Winnie himself. I didn't know he was in such a bad place. Had I known, I would have done something for him. The same goes for you. I should have written back to you all those times you wrote to me. Instead, I lost myself in a world of selfish self-pity. I am very sorry that I was not a good friend to you."

"I don't hold it against you, Tommy, this war changed us all. I was not surprised that you didn't write back to me. I was part of a past you no longer wanted to remember."

"But it was selfish of me," Tommy repeated. "I was thinking about how it made me feel, not about how much it would mean to you for me to speak to you. I was focusing on myself, instead of thinking of my duty towards others. But I am here now, and I intend to make amends."

"How can you possibly make amends?" Joseph asked. "There is nothing to make amends for. I do not feel resentment or anything else that we did not communicate for all those years. You owe me nothing."

"Just like you owe Winston Keats nothing, yet you took full blame and responsibility for a crime you didn't commit to save him."

Joseph had turned partly back towards them; he was glancing at Tommy from the corner of his eye with his head down, looking sheepish. He wasn't sure how to explain himself or what he had done. He had believed he was doing the right thing at the time. The only thing, in fact, that he could do.

"How did you learn about Keats?"

"We have access to the police archives," Clara explained. "We looked through them and we found that the police had a list of names of former employees for the tobacco shop. Two names stood out; Martin Lane and Winston Keats. Mr Lane does not appear to have any connection to the tobacco shop and there is no reason to suppose he was involved in the robbery, which is why we then went to meet Winston Keats. The address in the police file was for his mother's home and she told us the whole story."

"She was supposed to say nothing," Joseph said gruffly.

"She feels bad about your VC," Tommy added. "And I might have helped persuade her that it was in Keats' best interest if she told us the truth. A man cannot have his crimes ignored, Joseph, you know that as well as I do. While taking the blame for him was noble, it won't in the long-term help Winnie. If he had committed this crime then he must also take responsibility for it."

"You've met him, you've seen that he wouldn't survive prison," Joseph was furious.

"That's not the point," Tommy persisted. "Perhaps if it had become public knowledge that he was accused of the crime, and the personal suffering he was enduring was recognised, then he would have received help sooner rather than later? In any case, Keats is denying he committed the crime, and I am inclined to believe him."

"But the money!" Joseph shook his head at Tommy. "He suddenly had money which he could not have obtained in any other way than by robbing the tobacco shop."

"Keats claims that he was gifted that money," Clara said. "He says it arrived at his home in an envelope addressed to him and he even gave us the envelope. I also believe him."

"But, if that is true, what you are saying is that there is a third person out there, the true culprit," Joseph stared at them in disbelief. "You are saying that I went to prison not for the sake of Winston Keats but for this other person who appears to have gotten away with the entire crime!"

"They might have avoided the police and being sent to prison," Clara pinned him with her gaze, "but they didn't benefit from their crime, seeing as they sent what must have been most of the money to Winston Keats in an effort to shift the blame onto him. I imagine when the police became involved they panicked and sent him the money so they could accuse him of the crime if it became necessary to avoid the guilt being placed on themselves. They could never have predicted that you would take the blame before that occurred."

"If you had denied robbing that tobacco shop," Tommy now took up the thread of the story, "then the police would have investigated deeper, and our real culprit fancied they might get too close to the truth. They got rid of the money as quickly as they could, not only disposing of a vital piece of evidence, but shifting the blame."

"Then I wasted three months of my life in prison for nothing," Joseph was appalled by the realisation. "I ended up protecting someone who I never intended to protect, someone who deserved the sentence I suffered."

"That is how it looks," Clara admitted, trying to sound sympathetic. "Why don't you tell us in detail as much as you can about the police investigation? Maybe there is something they said to you during your questioning that could give us insight into who is really responsible."

Joseph considered for a second or two, then he looked confused.

"The police didn't say much at all. I learned of the robbery the day after it had occurred. I went to work as usual, and that was when Mrs Greaves told me about it. At the time I said how awful it was and didn't give it much more thought. Then she mentioned the police had asked for past names of those who had worked at the shop. I idly asked her who those people were and whether she believed any of them could have been responsible for this crime. That was when she listed to me the names she had told the police. I was mortified when she mentioned Winston Keats. I had been keeping contact with Winnie for some time, and I knew full well that he was in a bad place, and I truly believed him capable of anything. I decided the only thing I could do was visit him and try to get to the truth without alerting him to what I was about.

"I visited his mother first, and she was the one who mentioned to me that Winnie suddenly had come into a good deal of money. The second I heard that I was alarmed. I told her what I had just learned about the robbery at the tobacco shop, and she immediately came to the same conclusion as me. She had been deeply worried about where Winnie had suddenly obtained all this money from. My concerns merely confirmed what she had already feared – that Winnie had obtained it illegally. We discussed the matter for a while and became utterly convinced that Winnie had robbed that shop.

"In hindsight, we painted a bleaker portrait of him than was fair, but he was in such a dark place at the time and how else would he have gotten the money? That was when we came up with the plan. I persuaded Mrs Keats that I would take the blame for the crime. I would be able to survive prison far better than her son. She took some persuading but finally agreed. We mentioned nothing to Winnie, we thought it was best if he didn't know what we were about.

"Not long after that the police came knocking on my door. Turned out I was their prime suspect because I had recently started working at the tobacco shop. I got the impression that Mrs Greaves had pointed the finger at me, but I didn't hold that against her, after all she had been through a trying time. I suppose it would seem logical to accuse the man who had so recently been employed at the shop. I didn't deny anything, but I didn't admit to anything either, eventually the police decided I must be responsible and arrested me. The rest, I suppose, you know. I was held at the police station, questioned again, once more I refused to say anything in my defence, and eventually I was taken to court where I pleaded guilty."

Joseph came to a halt, the eerie apathy that had infested him before had now lifted as he contemplated the sacrifice he had made for someone he didn't know. He was scowling and clenching his fists when he spoke again.

"I went to prison for the person who was trying to frame my friend! Someone who I had no reason to protect at all!"

"We will find this person," Clara promised him in an effort to calm his rage." It has to be someone who is close enough to Mrs Greaves that they knew what was happening with the police investigation and became afraid it would be realised what they had done. Someone who decided to sneak the money to Winston instead. How much money did Mrs Greaves usually keep in her safe?"

"I wouldn't know precisely," Joseph answered. "However, it was at least upwards of £20. It had been a good week in the shop, and she had recently taken two orders for expensive cigar cases. Those had both gone out in the same week, and it had topped up the money in the safe considerably. Funnily enough, I had mentioned to Mrs Greaves the night before the robbery that it might be a good idea to bank the money sooner rather than later. She had told me that she always did her banking on a Friday, and nothing was going to change that. She swore to me the safe was perfectly sound."

"That would have been another nail in your coffin when the police came to question you," Tommy aired his thoughts aloud. "It would have seemed as though you were taking inventory of the money in the safe."

Joseph simply shrugged. He had made the remark in all innocence, merely trying to help the woman, that it had been used against him was not his fault.

"Who else would have known about the money in the safe?" Clara asked. "We have been through the list of names of those who formerly worked at the shop. We have ruled them out. That leaves you, Joseph, Mrs Greaves, and her son."

"Stuart has no reason to steal the money," Joseph replied. "His mother gives him a sizeable allowance. I have never seen the man want for anything, even if he is just a layabout. I suppose I shouldn't be so rude about him, but he used to get on my nerves just doing nothing and floating about at the back of that shop, saying he was going to become an engineer when we all knew he was just sitting around reading books and magazines."

"It is starting to look impossible," Tommy spoke. "We're running out of suspects."

"We simply haven't found the right suspect," Clara assured him. "But we will very soon. We need to go back to the police and see if there's anything else they can offer us."

Clara pulled the envelope out of her pocket and showed it to Joseph.

"Do you recognise the handwriting?"

Joseph shook his head over the envelope.

"You have to remember I wasn't working at the shop for very long before the robbery occurred, another thing that went against me. I do hope you can find out who did this sooner rather than later and clear my name. Now I know that Winnie wasn't responsible, I want my innocence proven and my good name restored. And I want my VC back. I am not taking the blame for someone else, someone who does not deserve my pity."

Joseph's anger was palpable, he had risen up from where he had been leaning against the table and was almost trembling with the outrage bubbling inside. Tommy wondered what exactly he would do if he did ever find out who was truly responsible for the robbery?

"We will do everything we can," Tommy reassured him. "We just have to figure out who else knew of that safe."

Clara was thinking about how a secret could end up not being so secret anymore. She was starting to see a possibility forming in her mind, but as yet it was only speculation. They had other things they had to investigate first before she could be sure that her suspicion was correct. But if she was right, then maybe – just maybe – there was a way that someone else could know about the safe who had not worked in the shop. And if that was the case, then the suspect list would suddenly have grown considerably.

Chapter Seventeen

There was no option but to return to the tobacco shop and speak once again to Mrs Greaves. Maybe, if they asked the right questions, she would reveal some clue that would help them to determine who had truly robbed her?

When they reached the tobacco shop, however, they were surprised to see that Mrs Greaves was not behind the counter. Instead, her son Stuart was standing manning the fort, looking utterly bored and fed up with the task and preferring to be anywhere else rather than there.

"You are in charge of the shop today?" Clara asked him, quickly overcoming her disappointment that she would not be able to speak to Mrs Greaves.

Stuart was flicking through a magazine; from the pictures Clara could see as he flipped the pages, it appeared to be one on the subject of motorcars. He leaned on the counter, a sour expression on his face that Clara did not think was specifically because she had walked in through the door. She fancied he would give the same look to everyone who tried to buy tobacco from him.

Clara guessed that Mrs Greaves would not have left her son in charge of the shop unless it was completely necessary.

"Mother had to go out," Stuart said without looking up from his magazine. "If you are concerned that I don't know how to cash up or count out the change correctly you can double check it before you leave."

With that surly remark Stuart proceeded to ignore them both.

Clara glanced at Tommy, wondering if there was any point continuing this conversation. Then again, despite what Joseph had said, if there was anybody who was in a prime position to steal from the safe it would be Stuart. Just because Joseph said Stuart had a sizeable allowance, didn't mean he wasn't short of money.

Clara decided against just walking away and waiting for his mother to return, instead she would ask Stuart a few questions; if he did not care to answer them, so be it. Maybe that would tell her everything she needed to know?

"You recall I was here previously, asking your mother about the robbery last year?" She began.

Stuart finally took a good look at them, abandoning his magazine for the time being and narrowing his eyes in their direction.

"Oh, it's you again. Mother said you were asking questions about the robbery and Jospeh Nunn."

"I wonder, Stuart, if *you* could give us a bit more information about the robbery?"

Clara took a few paces towards him and rested her hands on the shop counter before him.

"Why do you want to know about that?" Stuart grumbled. "You upset my mother asking about it the other day. She was all flustered afterwards and kept going on about it. Drove me to distraction. I don't know why you are so interested in a matter that is all over and done with."

"New evidence has come to light," Clara told him carefully. "It would seem that the gentleman who was found guilty of the robbery was not guilty at all."

"The fellow pleaded guilty to the charges," Stuart said in exasperation.

It was the first time they had seen him become somewhat animated. Whether this was a sign that he knew something about the robbery or whether he was simply frustrated with their line of questioning was not obvious.

"Yes, he did plead guilty at the time for his own personal reasons," Clara continued. "However, now he is aware of the new evidence we have uncovered, he is protesting his innocence."

"He can't do that, can he?" Stuart glanced between the two of them suddenly no longer interested in his motoring magazine. He looked perturbed.

"He certainly can," Tommy explained. "And because the money was never discovered it gives the police a reason to believe him. There was never any trace of the cash he stole nor, for that matter, any indication that he had spent it."

"Do you know how much was in the safe that day it was robbed?" Clara asked next.

"About £25," Stuart answered immediately. "I know that because my mother was going on about it for weeks afterwards. It had been a good week before the robbery, we had sold a couple of large cigar boxes that had been imported for some very particular customers. That sort of money doesn't come easily to us and to see it vanish like that was devastating. Even more devastating was the thought that someone we employed had taken it. Do you know how hard it has been on my mother? All these years working here by herself. It took me forever to convince her to employ someone to allow her a break from the shop, and then the first person she does employ goes and robs her! She won't employ anyone again."

"Some might wonder why you don't work in the shop more?" Tommy asked him with a stern expression.

"That is because I am studying to be an engineer," Stuart told him snootily. "That takes up all of my time and I simply cannot be in this shop helping out my mother. I am trying to better myself, to make a better life for us both, where we don't have to rely on this damn shop."

Stuart waved a hand vaguely around at the shelves of cigars, loose tobacco, and cigarettes.

"Did you believe that Joseph stole the money?" Clara tried a slightly different angle to get information from him.

"I trusted the police to have managed to find the right fellow," Stuart responded. "I had no opinion on Mr Nunn's guilt one way or the other, except to be disappointed he had proven himself such a cad."

"Where were you on the day of the robbery?" Tommy asked next.

Stuart cast him a fierce glance; he was clever enough to surmise that Tommy was wondering if he might have stolen the money.

"I was not here," he told them with a defiant look on his face as if he dared them to suggest he was the thief. "I was out with my girlfriend."

"Might we have her name so we can double check this?" Clara asked him.

"No, you may not," Stuart barked back at her. "I am done with all this. What business is this of yours anyway? This is a matter for the police. If you are not actually going to buy any tobacco I suggest you go on your way."

It was quite obvious that Stuart was not going to assist them any further. Despite his bad manners and his foul temper, Clara said thank you before she left as she always felt it was prudent to be polite. They headed out of the shop, none the wiser for their attempt to question Stuart, and paused on the pavement outside to consider what to do next.

"He is as likely a suspect as any," Tommy remarked to his sister.

"That is true, but without proof we might as well say the postman did it."

They had had finally come to an agreement that they would head for the police station and try their luck with Inspector Park-Coombs, when they spotted Mrs Greaves walking up the road. Her shoulders were slumped under an old shawl, and she carried a basket with both her hands as if it weighed a ton. Her head was down, half buried beneath the hat she was wearing, but they recognised her, nonetheless.

"I wonder where she has been?" Clara said quietly to Tommy. "She struck me as someone who wouldn't leave her shop without there being a very good reason for it."

As Mrs Greaves drew closer, Clara stepped forward and wished her good morning. The woman looked up sharply in surprise.

"Oh my, I did not see you there at first, you took me a little by surprise."

"We were just popping in to speak to you again," Clara said, smiling at her. "Could I take that basket for you? You look quite worn out."

Mrs Greaves fumbled with the basket in her hands. Clara had not lied when she said the woman looked worn out. Her face had a greyish pall to it and the basket, though it was empty, seemed too heavy in her hands. However, she hesitated to allow them to assist her.

"I am almost home," she nodded to the shop which was just a few paces away. "I shall be glad to get inside and have a cup of tea and then get on with the rest of my day."

"Please do let us assist you," Tommy said, moving forward and delicately slipping his hand around her elbow.

As he did so, he noted how thin and scrawny she was beneath the layers of clothes she was wearing. She felt as if she was nothing but bone beneath his fingers.

"Stuart will help me as soon as I get to the door," Mrs Greaves shook Tommy off. "I shan't detain you any longer."

She moved off firmly, trying to pretend nothing was the matter. Quite plainly, she didn't want to speak to them.

"Joseph Nunn says he's innocent," Clara remarked as the woman moved past her.

Mrs Greaves came to a sharp stop a few paces away from them. She stood stock still, refusing to turn around and face them.

"Does he now?" She said, her voice a little shaky.

"He thought he knew who had really stolen the money, and he was so worried about them going to prison, that he took the blame for them. It was easy enough to fool the police, they didn't look much further than Joseph. Now we know that the person who Joseph thought was responsible was innocent too, and Joseph took the blame for no reason, he wants his name to be cleared."

Mrs Greaves didn't budge an inch. Her body was so rigid she could have been a statue that had been stood in the middle of the pavement.

"We wanted to see if you could offer us any further details about the robbery," Tommy added.

All of a sudden Mr Greaves lost her grip on the basket and it dropped from her hands.

"Oh bother!"

Tommy moved quickly forwards and picked up the basket. He went to hand it back to her, which was when he realised Mrs Greaves had not dropped the basket out of shock but because her frail hands had suddenly spasmed and were now clamped into clawed shapes that prevented her from taking the basket back.

Clara drew to the opposite side of the woman, while Tommy checked the basket to see if the contents were damaged. They both noted how unwell the woman looked, as if a transformation had come over her while they were talking.

Mrs Greaves had no strength left in her body, not even the strength to hold a shopping basket. By waiting a moment to hear them out, she had expended the very last of her energy and been overcome.

"You are rather unwell I take it?" Clara placed a hand on her shoulder, trying to soften the blow of what was an otherwise very blunt question.

Clara was a firm believer that the direct approach was the best approach, though some would argue she would benefit from learning to be a bit more tactful.

"It's the winter, takes it out of you."

"I would say it's a touch more than just the winter," Clara responded.

Mrs Greaves shook her head and then glanced at Tommy who still had her shopping.

"Everything seems to have survived," Tommy smiled at her. "Let me carry the basket back to the shop for you."

Before Mrs Greaves could protest again, he was walking towards the front door of the shop and Clara had inserted her arm through the woman's to give her support as they headed to the door. Mrs Greaves seemed frustrated by the attention, but she didn't argue as she was led to the shop and shown inside.

Stuart glanced up the second the shop bell rang and was not pleased to see the return of Tommy and Clara. The next instant his eyes went to his mother and the sight of her clearly alarmed him. He dived along the counter, flipped up the service hatch and rushed towards the woman.

"Mother? Are you all right?"

He took hold of her by the upper arms and looked her straight in the face, his deep anxiety for her wellbeing apparent.

"I'm just a bit tired," Mrs Greaves brushed him off and walked behind the counter.

Before he could say anything more, she had gone through the doorway into the backroom and closed it behind her.

Stuart spun on Clara and Tommy, looking as though he was going to give them an earful about his mother. Perhaps he thought they had said something to her to upset her, and in that regard he wouldn't be wrong. Mrs Greaves had clearly been upset when they had mentioned to her that Joseph Nunn was now protesting his innocence. Before Stuart could say anything, Tommy thrust the shopping basket at him.

"Your mother dropped this," he said sharply to the younger man. "She does not seem well enough to be going out and doing her shopping by herself."

"She was perfectly well when she left the shop," Stuart snarled at him, grabbing the shopping basket, and rattling the contents in the process.

"You might need to start thinking about her a little more," Tommy told him gravely. "Maybe your mother is putting on a brave face for you? Perhaps it is time you started taking responsibility for this shop and for your future."

"That is exactly what I am doing by aiming to become an engineer."

Stuart wagged a finger at Tommy, daring him to question his plans. Tommy said nothing more and turned to leave with his sister. Back out on the pavement again, they started to walk through a light fog that was rolling in as the morning was drawing into the afternoon. The temperature seemed to have dropped several degrees, and they wouldn't be surprised if there was snow on the horizon.

"While I was checking the shopping basket to see if anything had been broken," Tommy said to his sister, "I noticed a medicine bottle with the name of a doctor on it."

"Then Mrs Greaves is very unwell," Clara said thoughtfully.

"More to the point if she is having regular appointments with a doctor, we both know how expensive that is."

"It would not make any sense for Mrs Greaves to steal from herself to pay for a doctor, that wouldn't achieve anything," Clara reminded him.

"No, that is true, but supposing we look at this a different way. Supposing the whole story about a robbery was not the truth. Supposing Mrs Greaves is trying to keep her illness a secret from her son, and she didn't want him seeing how much money she was spending on doctors' appointments and medicines? He knew about the £25 that was in the safe. Then it vanished. Maybe he started asking where it had gone, and Mrs Greaves panicked and said it had been stolen. That way she could hide from him that she was spending all this money on a doctor and thus hide her sickness."

"And once the ball got rolling, and the police were involved, then everything just got away from her. Joseph Nunn was accused and didn't deny it, and Mrs Greaves felt stuck because if she told the truth she would reveal what she was trying to keep such a secret from Stuart."

Clara considered this for a while.

"I am not sure it makes sense of all the evidence," she replied at last. "On the other hand, I do think it would be a good idea to pay a call to Mrs Greaves' doctor."

Chapter Eighteen

Annie was restless at home.

Normally she had so much to do during the day that she didn't have time to think about anything else, and with her recent activities meaning she had neglected her usual chores she had plenty to keep her occupied as she caught up with the housework. But nothing could truly distract her from thinking about Mr Maguire and the mystery that was building around him. As she cleaned out the chickens, shooing away Pip and Bramble who tried to get their noses into the coop and see if there were any eggs to steal, all she could think about was the late Mr Mullins and the strange paperwork she had found in his house.

When she went into the kitchen and began cleaning out the range, her mind was on whether Gilbert McMillan had found anything to prove that Maguire was bribing a planning officer. The letter they had found was certainly condemning but without a direct reference to Maguire, it was hardly helpful. The more Annie thought about things, the more she lost her confidence about the situation.

The day before she had been so sure they had nailed Maguire. That they had finally figured out what was going on and how to prove he was the scoundrel they had suspected, now she was becoming worried. Would he not simply place the blame for the bribery onto Mullins? Say that he was an innocent dupe in the scheme? With Mullins dead, it would be easy enough for him to take the blame for all of the corruption and scheming.

Maguire could end up looking like even more of a victim than before.

Annie was changing the sheets on the bed upstairs when she heard a knock on the front door. Bramble scurried to the door and began his frantic barking to alert the whole household that there was someone there. Annie wandered down the stairs and shuffled him away into the front parlour so she could open the door without him scooting out to greet the visitor. Sometimes people would be alarmed when they heard the sharp barking from within and would be startled when a small poodle sprang out at them. Those that were not used to dogs would sometimes shriek or jump back in surprise (even, occasionally, male visitors). Fortunately, Bramble was not an aggressive dog, he just liked to let people know he was there. Once the door was opened and he could see who the intruder was, he was quite happy to jump up on his hind legs and greet them as if they were an old and trusted friend. As a guard dog Bramble was not much use, for that matter Pip was little better. Neither of them would do much in the way of attacking someone who was about to cause trouble, more inclined to hide under the kitchen table and wait for Annie to sort out the difficulty.

As it happened, the person on the doorstep was Gilbert, he was red in the face from marching through the cold and was puffing out loud breaths that fogged before his lips. He nodded at Annie and gave his usual quirky grin.

"You look frozen to death," Annie said moving back so he could come into the hallway. Bramble burst out of the parlour and greeted Gilbert enthusiastically, bouncing up at his knees to get his attention.

Absentmindedly, Gilbert stroked the poodle's fluffy topknot. Bramble was usually clipped short to keep his coat neat and tidy, and because Tommy wasn't keen on the fancy poodle clips you saw in show rings, but the cold weather meant that a little bit of extra coat was beneficial, especially as Bramble could shiver on a warm, sunny day if the mood took him.

"Come through to the kitchen. I will make you a cup of tea," Annie told Gilbert leading the way to her private domain.

Annie was not sure if this was the first time that Gilbert had actually been in their house, she was trying to recall if she had ever fed and watered the journalist in the past. If she had, she had clearly eradicated the memory, consigning it to a part of her mind where she wouldn't have to ever think about it. There was something disagreeable about the thought of Gilbert being in their house, as if the neighbours might suddenly wonder what Annie was up to.

Gilbert managed to 'lower the tone' of a place just by his presence even though he did make occasional efforts with his appearance. Gilbert's clothes were of decent quality, and though his shoes were well-worn, they were usually polished. There was just something about him that made people feel that it was simply by a fluke of fortune he had become a journalist rather than a criminal.

"I assume you have news for me?" Annie asked as she began to make a pot of tea.

"You are quite right I do," Gilbert sat down at the kitchen table.

Pip had finally decided to come over and see who their guest was. She usually allowed Bramble to deal with the initial greeting of a visitor and then came out when she was satisfied that the person was dog friendly. Pip could get very disheartened if someone didn't like dogs and spoke to her harshly. Satisfied that Bramble had braved matters first and broken the ice, she now wandered over and rested her head in Gilbert's lap. Gilbert started to rub her behind the ears, and she was content to remain there.

"I think I know who the planning officer is who was prepared to take a bribe concerning Maguire's land," Gilbert said without preamble.

"That was fast," Annie said spinning around from the range.

"To be honest, as soon as I saw the letter I had a good hunch who it would be. There's been a certain person within the council offices who I have had suspicions about for a while. Until now, I haven't had any means to prove my suspicions. Then we found that letter and at long last I have something I can wave at this particular person and hopefully get them to speak to me."

"Corruption is serious business, especially when it involves someone who is in public service. Shouldn't we take it immediately to the police?"

"You have to be careful with these things," Gilbert tilted his head to one side as he explained. "You never know how deep these things run, or who has whom in their pocket."

"If you are suggesting that Inspector Park-Coombs would support someone who was corrupt and taking bribes then you are sorely mistaken."

"I would never denigrate your favourite inspector," Gilbert gave his cheeky smile. "However, there could be others further up in the force, or for that matter, within the council who might be involved and would use their clout to prevent any charges being brought. What you have to ask yourself Annie, is what matters to you the most at this moment in time? Rooting out a corrupt public official or dealing with

Maguire."

"I feel like the matter shouldn't be one or the other," Annie said. "It ought to be both."

"Life doesn't always work out that way," Gilbert shrugged at her. "But do you want to go speak to this particular official or not? I am going to go and wave this letter in front of him today and see what he has to say. You never know, we might get some information out of him concerning Maguire."

"And afterwards we can give the letter to the police," Annie said feeling it was her civic duty to enable the police to deal with a man who was breaking the law.

"You really want to leave this to the police to handle?"

Annie considered this for a moment, trying to assuage her own conscience about the matter. She wondered how Clara did this on a regular basis? How did she work out what the best thing to do was, whether to help the individual or society at large?

"You have to remember, Annie, that at this moment in time we don't have a strong link between Maguire, Mullins and this corrupt official," Gilbert added. "All the letters were addressed to Mullins, and while he was clearly Maguire's business partner - and it could be argued that Maguire must have known what was going on – a good lawyer could argue that Maguire was an innocent dupe in the whole affair."

"I have been worrying about that myself," Annie responded. "I keep thinking, what if Maguire squiggles out of this? We have to be so certain we can nail him."

"Exactly, so we are agreed we need more evidence before we hand this over to the police. Are you going to come with me when I go to speak to this planning officer?"

Annie hesitated for only a moment more, then nodded her head. She was in too deep now to leave things alone.

They didn't make a move until after she had served Gilbert the cup of tea she had promised, and he was warmed through again. Then they headed out, leaving the dogs at home to await the return of Tommy and Clara. Annie wondered what her husband and sister-in-law would make of the house being empty when they returned home. What would they say if they knew she was wandering around the streets after a corrupt planning officer, abandoning her usual role in the house? She knew they didn't mind her having a life of her own, but they would certainly be curious as to what she was up to. Annie was a creature of habit; Tommy had already noted that she was behaving differently. How long could she keep this secret from him?

They caught the bus and made their way into town. Gilbert told her that they were heading directly to the council offices. She tried to pretend, as they sat on the bus, that she was not connected to him even though they had entered the bus together. She recognised a couple of the ladies who were sitting in the back seats and worried what they would make of Annie being in the company of such a fellow as Gilbert. Annie was deeply concerned about reputation and respectability. Clara might not be troubled about such associations, but they troubled Annie a lot.

All the time they were on the bus, Gilbert talked to her. Annie kept her head facing towards the window and made only short murmuring answers, as if he were a stranger who had just happened to sit beside her. They were coming up to one of the stops when, out of the corner of her eye, Annie realised one of the ladies from the back of the bus was wandering down the aisle towards them. Annie assumed she was about to get off at the next stop, but as the woman neared the seat where Annie was sitting she stopped.

Annie was next to the window and Gilbert was beside her in the aisle seat. As the woman came to a halt, Gilbert gave her his broadest of smiles. The woman gave him a searing glance back and then looked at Annie.

"Is this gentleman bothering you, Annie?" The woman demanded fiercely.

Annie felt instantly guilty; in her efforts to disassociate herself from Gilbert she had gone too far and now her friends thought she was being pestered by an unsavoury gentleman. Of course, Gilbert *did* look like the sort of gentleman who would pester a woman on the bus, but he didn't deserve to be thought of that way when he was wholly innocent. Not that Gilbert took it to heart; he was a journalist through and through and he was quite prepared to be seen as devious and untrustworthy if it got the job done.

"Oh no, he's not bothering me," Annie said quickly to the woman.

It was quite obvious such a simple explanation was not going to prevent the woman from continuing to interfere. She was still glaring at Gilbert as if he were about to murder them all.

"Gilbert works for the newspaper," Annie blurted out, she probably could have thought of something else to say but she wasn't a very good liar. The truth came far too easily to Annie's lips and trying to think up a fabrication when she was already on the back foot was almost impossible. "Don't you remember, Gilbert did that report on the scone competition a couple of years ago?"

Annie threw in this detail in the hopes that it would distract the woman from wondering why Annie was suddenly associating with this man. The woman was the sort of person who considered it unspeakable to say good morning to a journalist, let alone to sit on a bus with one.

"Pleasure to meet you," Gilbert took his hat off and nodded his head to the woman. "Mrs Fitzgerald is kindly assisting me with an article. It is about old recipes you see, and Annie has said she can show me a section in the library which has a lot of information that will be useful to me."

Annie couldn't believe that Gilbert was assisting her, especially as he must have worked out that she didn't want anybody knowing that they were conspiring together or considering that they could potentially be friends. She felt even more ashamed of herself, now that he was helping her to mask the fact she was embarrassed to be with him.

"An article on old recipes?" The woman raised an eyebrow at her.

"Actually it's got more to do with Mr..."

Before Annie could even get to the end of her sentence Gilbert had jumped in.

"I recognise you! I was doing a follow up piece on the bonny baby competition, and it was your daughter who won it with your grandson. He was a smart looking little fellow in his blue bonnet."

The woman was disarmed by the flattery and the mention of the bonny baby competition. She soon began regaling them with anecdotes about her grandson, even taking the seat opposite Gilbert so that they could discuss things further. As a proud grandmother, she had been elated when her grandson had won the competition.

Annie didn't have to worry about trying to explain herself further, because Gilbert had completely distracted the woman from the situation and, when they finally arrived at their stop, the woman was so absorbed in the conversation she almost forgot that she was meant to be getting off the bus. They wished her goodbye as they finally parted company, Gilbert, and Annie walking in the opposite direction to her.

"I am very sorry Gilbert," Annie apologised as they were walking away. "I should have just been honest immediately when I saw my friend. I should not have tried to pretend that we were not working together."

Gilbert chuckled.

"I know you feel uncomfortable in my company, as if some of my seediness will rub off on you and tarnish your reputation."

Annie felt even worse at this statement.

"You have been nothing but kindness to me Gilbert and I should be more grateful to you and treat you better."

Gilbert waved off the remark.

"I am used to people looking at me as if I am something they stood in," he laughed. "It's part and parcel of being a newspaperman I don't take it to heart. Oh look there's the council offices."

Gilbert might not have taken the situation to heart, but Annie had. She felt terrible that she had treated him in such a manner. He deserved a good deal better after all the help he had given her. She might have said quite a few unpleasant things about Gilbert in the past, and she still had reservations about his questionable tactics, but he was assisting her freely and doing all he could to make sure that Clara and Tommy weren't found guilty of false defamation.

Annie resolved herself to do better by him. How could she hold her head up after this if she didn't at least try to be kinder to Gilbert?

From that moment on Annie promised herself she would no longer be embarrassed to be in his company, nor would she pretend that she was not with him if she saw her friends. It was time for Annie to turn over a new leaf and let go of some of her long-held prejudices.

Chapter Nineteen

As Gilbert and Annie headed into the council offices, the first person who greeted them was a receptionist sitting behind a large desk to one side of the tiled foyer. She was an older woman with a pair of spectacles she kept on a thin gold chain around her neck. She looked up with a smile on her face which immediately disappeared upon seeing Gilbert.

"Oh, it is you Mr McMillan," she said, raising one eyebrow at him in a disapproving fashion. "Who is it you wish to disturb today?"

Gilbert merely smiled wickedly at her, unperturbed by her demeanour or her gruff manner.

"I would be delighted to see Mr Florentine today."

"I am not sure he has the time to see you," the receptionist said gruffly.

Annie had the impression that no matter who Gilbert had said he wanted to see the response would have been the same.

"I think he will want to see me," Gilbert said nonchalantly. "Perhaps when you ring up on that internal telephone system you have, you will mention to him that I have recently been speaking to a gentleman by the name of Mullins. I think he will know what I mean."

The receptionist didn't look as though she was inclined to do anything, Gilbert, however, continued to smile at her, waiting patiently for her to move. This was a competition they had on a regular basis, with Gilbert being the perpetual winner. After nearly a minute of simply staring at each other, the receptionist finally gave in and picked up the telephone receiver next to her. She had not even glanced in Annie's direction, which the latter was rather glad for; she didn't want to be remembered by this frightening woman who seemed quite a harridan.

The woman spoke cautiously into the telephone, trying to whisper so Gilbert couldn't overhear what she was saying. When she mentioned the name Mullins she came to a sudden stop as if someone on the other end of the line had spoken sharply, causing her to hesitate. She was silent a moment, listening to the person on the other end of the line. Though she maintained a neutral expression on her face, she blinked rapidly as if taken by surprise, before glancing back in the direction of Gilbert. She was still looking bemused as she put down the telephone receiver.

"Mr Florentine asks if you could go up to his office at once?"

Gilbert thanked her heartily and motioned for Annie to follow him as he headed through another door and towards a staircase.

Annie had never been in the council offices before and was unaware of their grandeur until that day. They were housed in the town hall which had been designed to accommodate a lot of tall ceilings and marble furnishings, along with a grand staircase that swept up the wall as if they were in a stately home. Annie found herself looking around, mildly aghast at the extravagance of the building and unable to take it all in. When they climbed up the stairs they came to a landing with a towering window that must have been about ten feet in height. It was filled with a stained-glass design commemorating some historical figure from Brighton's past that Annie didn't recognise.

Annie was beginning to feel overwhelmed; she was out of her depth and feeling intimidated by the implications of power and money this place exuded. She was very glad Gilbert was 'leading the charge,' so to speak; he didn't appear to ever feel intimidated or out of his depth.

There was no place in this world that Gilbert didn't assume he would naturally fit into, or for that matter, a place where he fancied he should not go. Annie, on the other hand, was routinely anxious about going anywhere she had not been before simply because she was so concerned about being welcomed by whomever was there. Perhaps, Annie thought to herself, it was time she let go of some of those anxieties and instead started to be a little bit more carefree about what others thought of her?

They reached another landing and walked along it until they came to a door with a glass window. On the window, in black painted letters, was the name Mr Florentine. Gilbert did at least have the manners to knock on the door rather than waltz straight in uninvited.

There was a pause and then someone asked for them to enter.

Sitting behind a desk in the room was a small man with black unruly hair he had attempted to master by oiling it carefully into place. He rose from his seat and smiled at them in a friendly fashion, offering his hand to Gilbert at once and giving a polite bow to Annie. He had a narrow, slightly awkward face; his front two teeth overlapped a fraction, which should not have been really noticeable, but for some reason drew Annie's attention.

Mr Florentine might not be considered handsome, but in the right setting he could be deemed charming. This was *not* the right setting because he was clearly uneasy. A bead of sweat wobbled on his upper lip as he now turned to Gilbert, the smile becoming somewhat fixed.

"What is this about Mr Mullins?"

Mr Florentine's attempt to act as if the name meant very little to him immediately failed.

"We have been to Mr Mullins house," Gilbert said to him. "He's dead, you know?"

There was an immediate look of relief in Florentine's eyes which told them more than any words could. He visibly relaxed and started to sit down in the chair he had jumped up so keenly from when they had first entered. He remembered himself a moment later and motioned for them to take the seats opposite his desk.

"What a shame, do you know it seems as if I hear about someone I know passing away nearly every day. I wonder if it's due to my age? Everybody just keeps getting older and dying."

He was not doing a good job of distracting them or sounding as casual as he was attempting.

"Fortunately, Mr Mullins left plenty of paperwork behind," Gilbert was still as cheery as always. "Including a rather interesting letter. It mentioned specifically the planning permission that was needed for the building of those new bungalows down on the cliffs."

The smile froze on Mr Florentine's face, then it gradually drooped until he looked as though he was grimacing instead of smiling. He didn't say anything as Gilbert continued with his explanation.

"Quite a curious letter it was. It explained how planning permission might be declined because of concerns about the site being common land used for grazing. A lot of people complained about the proposal. However, it is good to know that with the right amount of persuasion you were perfectly able to see that permission was granted."

Gilbert might have hedged around the information in the letter, but Mr Florentine was fully aware of what he was saying. Until that point, Annie had only ever read in magazines about people gulping and had never realised it was something they actually did when they were nervous or upset. Mr Florentine now gulped, and Annie heard him noisily swallow. There was no longer a smile on his face, and he was having a hard time trying to find the words to counter Gilbert's discreet accusation.

"I believe you are accusing me of something Mr McMillan?"

"I should have thought that was fairly obvious," Gilbert laughed. "I'm accusing you of taking a bribe to push through the planning permission for those bungalows. You had the casting vote. I wonder what would have happened if those who wanted the site to remain common land for grazing had been aware that all it took was a good deal of money to have you vote in the appropriate fashion?"

"Your evidence that I took a bribe sounds flimsy," Florentine tried to drag himself out of the situation.

"Flimsy is a curious choice of words, when the letter states in black and white that you would be prepared to take a bribe to swing the vote."

Mr Florentine glanced in the direction of Annie suddenly, a desperate flicker in his eyes. If he thought he might receive some assistance from her, he was mistaken. Gilbert was on the attack, and Annie had no intention of stopping him.

"What would you care for me to say?" Mr Florentine added. "You already seem to have enough information."

"Bribery is a serious matter," Gilbert continued. "But, under the circumstances, there is something else we want to know about, or rather someone else. If you assist us in our inquiries we might be inclined to be more generous with what we do with the information in the letter afterwards."

Annie was appalled that Gilbert might be suggesting they would conceal the letter if Florentine helped them. She was about to protest when she saw Gilbert cast her a conspiratorial look out of the corner of his eye. He didn't move his head, but the brief glance told her he was up to something and that she should be quiet. Reminding herself that only a moment ago she had said she would start to think better of Gilbert, and not automatically assume he was up to something shifty and dishonest, she bit her tongue and didn't say anything.

"What can I do then?" Mr Florentine asked Gilbert eagerly. "I take it you want information?"

"We want to know about the connection between you, Mr Mullins, and Mr Maguire. We want to know how heavily involved in this bungalows scam Mr Maguire was."

"You're calling it a scam now?" Florentine looked unhappy.

"You must have seen all the surveys," Gilbert snorted at him, as if the man's attempt at innocence was ridiculous. "The land is not suitable for building upon, the surveyors stated that bluntly. It was bought cheaply under dubious circumstances and the land rights were ignored. Maguire planned on selling shoddily built houses fully aware that within a few years they would be crumbling to pieces. Taking money from people with false promises is what I call a scam, wouldn't you agree Mr Florentine?"

Florentine gritted his teeth together.

"You understand I had nothing to do with the rest of it, I was just involved in the planning permission. Whether the land is suitable for building on is not my concern. My only issue was whether there would be objections from the public concerning the land being used for such a thing."

"Objections you did not need much help to dismiss," Annie now interjected.

"The objections were laughable. While there were protests from several different individuals regarding the land being common ground for grazing, the council was split on whether they should be upheld. No one had actually used that grazing land in years, I don't think anybody remembers the last time there were sheep or cattle, or even horses, on it."

"Are you saying that even without the bribe you would have voted for the planning permission to go in Maguire's favour?" Gilbert asked him.

Florentine looked deeply uncomfortable at this question, unsure how he was supposed to answer. He cleared his throat.

"The situation was complicated, up to the point of the actual vote I was not sure which way I was going to go. However, the money that I was offered by Mr Mullins on the behalf of Mr Maguire was certainly enough to sway me. You appreciate I am admitting to nothing this is just between us."

Gilbert shrugged his shoulders, indifferent to what Florentine thought.

"What can you tell us about Mr Maguire's involvement?" Gilbert persisted.

"Only that he *is* involved and was fully aware of everything that was going on. He and Mullins went together to purchase the land with the view in mind that they would build properties and sell them quickly for a profit. The land was sold cheaply as no one thought anyone would ever build on it. I think there might have been some irregular dealings with the person who sold it, but that was none of my concern. As I say, there was nothing from a planning perspective, apart from the common land rights, that could have prevented permission being granted."

"Do you have anything you can give us that would prove that Maguire was responsible for this scam?" Annie now asked.

"I didn't precisely leave a paper trail that would have been stupid," Florentine snorted derisively in her direction. "I thought Mullins would have been sensible enough to burn that letter I sent him, but I didn't put my name on it, just to be safe."

"It didn't take a genius to work out which planning officer might have been responsible for such a thing," Gilbert smirked at him. "You have a reputation."

"As do you Mr McMillan, you are always poking about in my business."

"Because I always have grave concerns that you are up to no good."

"Stop, stop," Annie interrupted once more because it looked like the two of them were going to get into a mild slanging match. "What Mr Florentine did was dishonest and corrupt, but that is not the purpose of us being here. We are here because of Mr Maguire. We need to find a way to discredit him."

"Well, if you want any more proof from me I can't offer it to you. I did all my dealings with Mullins. I knew Maguire was involved but you won't get me to say that out loud. That would do me no good. It would simply mean that I would find myself accused of corruption."

He had a good point. It was not in Mr Florentine's best interest to stand up and accuse Maguire of doing anything.

"Well that's a shame," Gilbert said, starting to stand up. "You see, if you could have offered us something then I would have been inclined not to now go to the police and tell them what I know. But, as you cannot be helpful to us, I suppose I'll just have to go take that letter to them. I wonder how well things will go for you in terms of promotion through the council, or even retaining your job, if the police are looking at you for corruption?"

Florentine was immediately alarmed.

"Wait, I didn't have any dealings with Maguire but if you want to find out the truth about those building works and the scam he was involved in you ought to look into the person who he bought the land off in the first place. I happen to know their name because it was told to me by Mullins."

Florentine started to rummage in a drawer. He pulled out a notebook upon which he had made some scrawled jottings concerning a recent meeting.

"Mullins is truly dead?"

"It appears he had a heart attack," Annie responded.

Florentine considered this for a moment then went back to his notes.

"If you want to know more about Mr Maguire and about his dubious dealings you want to speak to a Miss Carter. She was the one who sold him the land and from my understanding she wasn't happy when she learned he was going to build upon it. She was at some of the council meetings when the planning was being discussed and I know she was in talks with some of the other planning officers and wanted them to deny the permission. I can give you her address because we keep the addresses of anyone who makes a formal protest against a planning application."

"Aren't those supposed to be private and confidential?" Annie asked him.

Florentine glanced in her direction.

"Look, I just want to stay out of this, do you want the address or not?"

"We want the address," Gilbert promised him. "And we want it right now."

Chapter Twenty

Mrs Greaves went to a doctor by the name of Cunningham. His address was not far from her tobacco shop, so it did not take them long to walk there. He had his surgery in an old Victorian mansion, renting the rooms on the ground floor of the right-hand side of the property. The floor above him was rented by a dentist and the rooms opposite were rented out respectively by a solicitor and an accountant. There were a series of brass plaques screwed to the front wall of the house just by the door which listed the names, occupations, and respective qualifications for the people within. After studying the plaques for a second or two, Clara entered through the front door and found herself in a small and snug reception area. An older man, leaning back in a chair in the corner, was clearly there to direct them to the respective person they wished to see and to prevent people wandering into the wrong section of the property. He had been reading the newspaper as they entered and looked as though he spent a good deal of his time propped in the corner asleep.

"Who would you be wishing to see today?" He asked them.

"We were hoping to speak to Dr Cunningham about one of his patients," Clara explained.

"Dr Cunningham is a very busy man, and I can't imagine him

having time to simply chat to someone who walks in off the street," the gentleman remarked. "But if you wish to remain here a second, I shall go speak to his receptionist and see if he is willing to see you."

The gentleman rose, leaving his folded newspaper on the seat of his chair and walked out of the snug foyer. The room had clearly been created when the property was split into a series of offices and the wall that blocked them from the rest of the hall was really just a wooden dummy wall with a door in the middle. They could hear the concierge's footsteps running behind it and, if they had listened hard enough, they would have heard his voice as he spoke to Cunningham's receptionist.

"What are the odds this doctor will even talk to us about Mrs Greaves?" Tommy said to Clara. "You know how doctors can be about talking about their patients."

Clara was well aware; She had been thinking about the matter as they had walked to this property. She knew it was a long shot getting the doctor to talk to them about Mrs Greaves.

She had so many questions for the man. He was clearly a doctor who cost a lot of money. Just looking around the reception area, you could tell he was a doctor who expected his clients to be of a certain calibre. Not a place you would expect to find a woman who ran a tobacco shop patronising.

Yet again it raised the question of how Mrs Greaves was affording to come here?

The concierge returned a few minutes later shaking his head at them.

"The doctor is far too busy this morning, but his receptionist says she has a slot free later this afternoon if you wish to come back. She says you will have to pay for it, however, as she can't simply give away a free appointment."

Clara hesitated, while all her expenses were technically paid by her client, which in this instance was Joseph Nunn's father, she didn't like to abuse his purse.

"How much does an appointment cost?"

"I believe the first consultation is £5, and then the rate is reduced significantly afterwards if you become a regular patient," the concierge explained.

Clara did her best not to pull a face. This doctor really was expensive; was she prepared to pay that sort of money for what might end up as wasted effort?

After tossing the thought back and forth for a while, she decided the doctor's prices probably weren't worth the cost. The chances were they would arrive at the appointment and the doctor would refuse to tell them anything about Mrs Greaves. Doctors could be rather particular about their patient's privacy, especially the expensive ones.

"We shall think on it and perhaps return another day," Clara told the concierge.

The gentleman gave them a nod as if he'd heard this response more than once and went back to his newspaper. Clara was about to leave when a new idea jumped into her mind. There was just a slim chance it might work but slim chances were Clara's speciality.

"I don't suppose you happen to know Mrs Greaves?"

The concierge put his head up and glanced at her.

"The lady who runs the tobacco shop?"

"The one and the same. I believe she was visiting Dr Cunningham today? On her way back to the tobacco shop she was overcome by a feeling of terrible weakness. She dropped her shopping basket, and looked like she might collapse. Luckily, we were nearby and helped her back to her home."

None of this was a lie, just an extension of the truth. To suggest

Mrs Greaves had been so unwell that she needed helping back to her shop was not so far from the truth, even if it had been the shock of seeing Tommy and Clara, rather than her illness, which had sparked her sudden indisposition.

The concierge reacted as Clara had hoped he might; he looked at her with an expression of deep concern.

"That is why you came to see the doctor?" He asked, suddenly seeing things in a new light. "Is she quite all right? Does she need someone to attend to her?"

"Mrs Greaves refused any further assistance," Clara said with complete honesty. "But I thought I would pop by and see if there were any medical suggestions the doctor would like me to relay back to her, or any additional medicine he would like her to have?"

"Of course, that is most considerate of you. I think I should speak to Dr Cunningham again, now I see the situation so much clearer."

The concierge got up, placing his folded newspaper on the seat of his chair, and headed back through the door and into the main portion of the building. Tommy gave his sister a look after he had gone.

"Well played."

"And completely honest. We are here out of consideration for Mrs Greaves' health."

"Among other things," Tommy grinned at her. "I wonder how she can possibly afford to come to this place? Though, it does explain why she might have been trying to hide from her son where that money was going to. Not just so he wouldn't know she was ill but that she was spending a small fortune on a doctor. I have a feeling Stuart is somewhat mercurial in his attitude towards the shop and his mother's finances, I can't imagine him being delighted to learn that the money that should have been going into the bank, and eventually into his inheritance, was instead being spent on a very expensive doctor."

"Stuart Greaves clearly doesn't intend to ever work for a living," Clara replied. "Whatever he says about studying to be an engineer, he is really just stalling for time. He is quite happy living off his mother. When she dies I imagine he's hoping she will have a substantial fortune set aside that he can simply continue to live upon."

"And what of his girlfriend? Do you believe she exists?"

"Oh, I believe she exists, and I wouldn't be surprised if she is a young lady of significant means. Another person that Stuart can live off rather than have to make a living for himself."

They brought their conversation to a quick stop when they heard footsteps returning; the concierge appeared a second later around the door of the foyer.

"Dr Cunningham says he can spare you a few minutes if you would kindly come this way."

Clara was somewhat impressed that her tactic had worked, especially as she had only improvised it at the very last moment. They followed the concierge through into the main portion of the house, along a grand hallway and passed a sweeping staircase running up the wall that formed the original entryway of the property. They were led to a door situated just behind the staircase. Framed on the wall beside this door was a notice that stated the name once again of Dr Cunningham. They went through the door and into a large salon which, once upon a time, must have been the scene of a great number of grand balls but now was set out as a waiting room. There was a prim looking middle-aged woman sitting behind a desk. She appeared to be waiting for them. The concierge went over to her and spoke quietly, nodding his head towards Clara and Tommy.

"Dr Cunningham says if you could go through he has a few moments for you," the receptionist repeated what the concierge had told them, motioning a hand to a door just to their left.

Clara and Tommy didn't waste any time waiting for further instructions, they went to the door, politely knocked and, when asked to enter, did just that.

Dr Cunningham was a man in his sixties, probably on the cusp of considering retirement. He dressed smartly and kept himself in shape, along with retaining a full head of hair which made him look dashing for his age. Clara could imagine that many of his female patients of a certain age would be rather besotted with him, especially when he stood up and beamed a charming smile at her.

"I am told there is an issue with Mrs Greaves?" He asked immediately without preamble. "Is she quite all right? She left my office only about half an hour ago."

"I think probably the cold got to her as she walked home," Clara explained. "We were fortunate to be just outside her shop when she was coming along the road. She looked quite unwell, I must admit, unlike the woman we had seen before in her shop. It wasn't until she dropped her shopping basket, and we helped her into her home, however, that we realised quite how much weight she had lost."

Clara threw this comment in to make it seem as if they had known Mrs Greaves for some time and were concerned friends. It was a good surmise that Mrs Greaves had lost considerable weight, as her clothes were clearly for a larger lady, and they had both been surprised to feel her bony arms.

Dr Cunningham motioned for them to take seats in front of his desk and sat down himself.

"Mrs Greaves is a very unwell woman," he agreed with them. "But I am not at liberty to speak much about her condition as she prefers others not to know, especially her son."

"We are aware of that," Tommy responded. "Stuart knows nothing about this."

"Indeed? I have told his mother that it would be advisable for her to speak to him sooner rather than later, but she completely refuses to do so. I suspect she is in denial of her real condition herself."

"Is she dying?" Clara asked, not certain the doctor would answer such a direct question.

Dr Cunningham took a moment to consider his answer before he spoke. Eventually he seemed to decide that someone else ought to know about Mrs Greaves' situation, and as Clara and Tommy appeared to be friends with the woman, he would prefer they knew that something was amiss and that she might need help in the future.

"She is not dying per se, she needs an operation. As long as the operation is undertaken and is successful then she should go on to live a long and full life."

"When is this operation occurring?" Tommy asked. "She will need someone to keep an eye on the shop and to distract Stuart."

He was playing up the notion that they were friends who would help Mrs Greaves in her hour of need. He felt slightly dishonest doing so, and tried to assuage his guilt by promising himself he would see if could not make some sort of arrangement for the poor woman.

"Mrs Greaves has yet to decide when she wishes to have the operation," Dr Cunningham explained. "We have discussed it repeatedly, but she cannot make up her mind."

"I have to say, doctor," Clara now interjected, "I was somewhat surprised to see that this was where Mrs Greaves was coming for medical advice. I had not supposed she could afford to see a doctor of your prestige. I am not begrudging your prices of course, I'm sure your services are worth it, but Mrs Greaves is not a wealthy woman nor someone who can simply throw around £5 for a consultation."

"You are quite right," Dr Cunningham nodded at her. "But I have an arrangement with Mrs Greaves. You see, she has supplied me with my favourite cigars and cigarettes for years and years. Due to that arrangement, when I learned that she was unwell and refusing to see a doctor because of the cost, I offered my services instead. I have not charged her a penny for anything, not even the medicine, the only thing she will have to pay for is the operation and even then I have said to her that I would be quite happy to subsidise her bill. I know she doesn't like to consider being a charity, but my offer is not that, it is a gesture of friendship."

That certainly explained how Mrs Greaves was able to afford such a doctor, it also put paid to the notion that she might have taken the money from the safe herself to spend on Dr Cunningham, while trying to keep it a secret from her son.

"I would appreciate it if you could have a quiet word with Mrs Greaves and try to convince her to book her operation sooner rather than later," Dr Cunningham persisted. "The longer she leaves it, the harder will be the recovery time, and there could come a point when her condition damages her health in the long term."

Clara sensed there was more than simply friendly concern in the doctor's manner. If she had to offer an opinion, she would suggest that the older doctor held a torch for the woman at the tobacco shop and that was why he was so keen to look out for her.

"We will do our best," Clara promised him. "Thank you for taking the time to speak with us. You have relieved some of our concerns regarding Mrs Greaves."

That was the full truth, even though those concerns were not quite the same as the ones the doctor had. Dr Cunningham wished them well and they left the surgery saying thank you to the concierge and receptionist as they headed back outside.

"Yet another dead end," Tommy said to his sister.

Clara didn't respond because she was deep in thought. Where

would they go next with this case? Who could they ask next? Things were becoming complicated and there was no obvious solution in sight.

"We need to figure out who would have had a connection to Keats to consider giving him that money after the robbery," she said at last. "That is the link that will help us to find the true criminal."

"Well, then where do you want to go next?" Tommy asked.

Clara smiled to herself.

"To the pub."

Chapter Twenty-One

The *Ruddy Mallard* was a quaint little pub set down a back street. It was the sort of place that visitors to Brighton in the summer would happily enter and pay a few pence for a pint of beer without feeling intimidated by the locals. Wealthy tourists would perceive it as a sanitised version of the colourful characters and decaying architecture to be found in the earthier pubs in the area. The *Ruddy Mallard* managed to toe the line between welcoming its regulars and attracting the respectable sightseer during the holiday season.

It was also Keats' favourite pub.

They were hoping to find people who were friendly with Keats and might be able to offer insight into the sudden wealth he came into. If the money had been an innocent gift, an act of charity by one of Keats' friends, or if it had been given to him deliberately to make him appear guilty of the robbery, the pub seemed a logical place to find a new lead. After all, it was the only place Keats went regularly, where someone would know of his current situation and also that he had formerly worked in the tobacco shop.

Clara and Tommy entered the pub and glanced around. It was early afternoon and there were not that many people present, though a couple of labourers were helping themselves to pints of beer, trying to take the chill out of their bones before they headed back to work. Behind the bar, a portly lady with her hair done up in neat curls efficiently polished clean beer mugs. She had a friendly smile and projected a welcoming aura that drew new patrons inside. She now turned this smile onto her two new customers.

"What can I get you two?"

They decided it would be impolite to fail to order a drink. Clara was not inclined towards beer, but Tommy was always happy to have a pint. He ordered one at once, while Clara noted that on a sign at the back of the bar there was a list of non-alcoholic drinks. She ordered a lemonade, and this was brought to her in a glass bottle with a little glass ball in the top that had to be popped out to enable the contents to be drunk. The landlady opened the bottle for her and there was a satisfying fizz to reveal the contents were carbonated and the glass stopper had done its work to prevent the fizz being lost.

Their arrival seemed to precede a sudden surge in custom and the landlady was swiftly distracted. They sipped their drinks and waited until the rush died down before attracting the landlady's attention again. She moved towards them, anticipating another drinks order. Clara did not waste time correcting this notion.

"We are friends of Mr Keats. We've popped in today to ask you a little bit about his current circumstances as we wish to help him."

The landlady was polishing the bar with a cloth, mopping up a spillage of beer created by another customer. She frowned at the mention of Keats.

"That poor young man, he really is lost in this world. He comes in here quite often. He would drink himself silly except I'm careful and I make sure to water down his pints."

"I served with Keats," Tommy explained. "Only briefly, before I was wounded and invalided home. I only recently learned that he had come back from the war so dreadfully damaged."

"So many men came back damaged beyond repair," the landlady nodded her head. "My own dear late husband was a shell of the man who went to war. He was gassed and never really recovered from it. Only a couple of years after the war, he passed away very suddenly from pneumonia. He should have been in the prime of his life but, well, the doctor said it was the result of the gas damaging his lungs in the war. His body was never the same."

As so often happened when they began discussing the war and those who had either not come back from it, or had come back terribly broken, a solemn silence fell over them all.

"Keats is in a very bad place," Tommy spoke. "I would like to help him, but I'm also rather concerned to learn that someone has been trying to use him."

The landlady now looked at him in surprise.

"What is this? Who has been doing this?"

"Someone tried to pin the tobacco shop robbery on him that happened last year," Tommy said, deciding full disclosure was the best approach to get the information they needed. "It is somewhat complicated, but the gentleman who eventually was found guilty of the crime only took the blame because he thought that Keats had done it, and he wanted to protect him. They were both men in my regiment, and I am very disheartened to hear what has occurred. As it turns out, Keats was not responsible either, someone was trying to set him up, thinking he was an easy target to take the blame. I am very angry about this, and I want to see that something is done to rectify the matter."

"What a terrible situation," the landlady gasped. "What a horrible thing to do to two young men. I don't know what this world is coming to. I am certain that ever since the war things have not been the same. People are so much more selfish these days, don't you find?"

"We're trying to work out who would have had a connection to Keats and the tobacco shop, and knew that he used to work there," Clara explained. "We know that Keats often drinks here, and we're wondering if you could tell us the names of some of the people who associate with him regularly? Perhaps there is someone in particular who was being very friendly with him around the time of the robbery last year but has subsequently lost interest in him."

The landlady's eyes narrowed.

"People can be so terrible," she said, tutting to herself. "Befriending a poor lost soul like that young man and using him for their own nefarious means. I feel awful about it myself. I try to keep an eye on him, knowing that he is such a lost little soul. I think of how his mother must feel knowing that he is out here in the world all alone, struggling to get by. I clearly have not been doing as good a job as I thought I was."

"You could hardly be expected to keep an eye on him all the time, nor could you be expected to keep the woes of this world away from him," Clara consoled her. "Can you think of anyone who may have befriended him recently? They might have seemed an unlikely person to associate with Keats?"

The landlady's frown deepened.

"I'm afraid nobody springs to mind. The young man comes in here on his own and he generally sits by himself. He likes that corner by the fireplace."

She pointed to the spot she had mentioned where there was a bench seat running along the wall between a fireplace and the corner of the room. It was a quiet nook hidden away from the rest of the world.

"There are a few fellows who will pass the time of day with him, but no one who I would consider a close friend."

"Perhaps we should come back at a later hour and meet some of these gentlemen who will pass the time of day with him?" Tommy suggested. "They might be able to offer us something more."

"Indeed they might," the landlady smiled at him. "I can easily point them out to you if you want to come later this evening. Keats usually comes in around four in the afternoon and stays until I close. I would like to see him getting some help, it would be nice to think that he could have a better life than what he is currently living. He seems such a nice young man, deserving of so much more."

Clara concurred with the lady's sentiment. Keats did seem to deserve more than what life had so far given him and she was hopeful that once this case was resolved they would be able to help restore him to the life he should have.

The landlady excused herself as new customers had just come in. They were a well-dressed couple who appeared to be visitors coming to the *Ruddy Mallard* to soak up the atmosphere. Clara imagined that part of the reason the landlady made sure she had non-alcoholic drinks on the menu was because she frequently received visitors just like them. The sort who treated her pub as if it were an attraction, much like the zoo. A place where they could observe the labouring classes at a safe distance.

But perhaps that was too harsh an assessment. Clara could be excessively cynical at times.

The landlady was quickly absorbed taking the order of her new customers. Tommy and Clara finished their own drinks, took one last look around the pub, and then departed.

"It has to have been someone who met him in the pub," Clara said to her brother once they were outside and walking back towards the bus stop.

"I agree, so we shall come back here later this evening?"

"Absolutely, we have to figure this out, one way or the other."

With only a few hours to waste before they could make a return to the pub, it made better sense for them both to go to Tommy's house. Clara saw no point heading all the way to her own home, only to immediately turn around and head back. As soon as she was through the familiar front door, Clara telephoned Captain O'Harris and explained to him where she was and her plans for the evening, with the suggestion he might care to join them on their adventure. Having heard the bare bones of their case, O'Harris immediately agreed that he would meet them at the Fitzgerald house and accompany them back to the pub that evening.

Clara was pleased as she liked to spend as much time with her husband as she could, and they had been somewhat apart these last few days. O'Harris was busy with work at the home and hadn't been able to accompany her on this particular case. Being able to unite again for an evening in the pub, even if it was while working a case, would be pleasurable.

"I would ask Annie to accompany us too," Tommy said from the kitchen where he had been letting the dogs outside. He was now offering them some scraps of ham as an apology for not taking them with him that day.

"But I just can't seem to find her."

Clara joined him in the kitchen. She was surprised to see that the room, which was normally a hive of activity, was oddly quiet. Usually, at this time of the day, Annie was preparing things for the evening meal or cooking something for lunch. There was almost always something baking in the oven, whether it was a cake, scones, or some other floury delight. Today there was no cooking, no prepping and, more to the point, the range was cold. Annie rarely let the range go cold because it was a pain to light it again and bring it up to a decent temperature. But when Clara looked in the little door at the fire, she saw that though it had been left banked up, it had burned out at least a couple of hours ago, allowing the whole metal range to grow cold. Annie would be furious when she got back, it would take her ages to get the temperature just how she liked it to suit her baking.

"What is your wife up to Tommy?"

"Beats me," Tommy shrugged his shoulders, his hands in his pockets as he leaned against the table. "Something is on her mind, and she's been disappearing at all hours during the day. She hasn't said anything to me about what she is doing. I am starting to feel a little hurt that she is keeping secrets."

A sudden thought came to Clara, a possibility as to why Annie had abandoned the house and her husband and neglected her usual schedule.

"She wouldn't be going to see a doctor would she?"

"Annie isn't ill," Tommy said with alarm in his voice.

"You don't just go to a doctor when you are ill," Clara told him with a knowing look.

"What? Oh, no if Annie was... If Annie was that way, she would have definitely spoken to me first."

"It was just a thought. It has to be something very important to make her neglect her kitchen and, as Annie seems fit and healthy in every other regard, it was the only thing I could think of."

Tommy was uncomfortable discussing this aspect of his marital life.

"I'm sure if there was anything going on she would have mentioned it to me by now. Knowing Annie there is probably a cooking competition she is keeping under wraps."

Clara was unconvinced. Annie was not the sort of person to act nefariously, or secretively, unless there was a very good reason for it.

"She will be home shortly, no doubt," Tommy added, since his sister had not responded and was making him uneasy by how deeply she was contemplating the situation.

Tommy and Annie had been married over a year and had been indulging in all the usual activities that a married couple enjoyed. Yet nothing had come of their nightly shenanigans, which was something of a surprise to both of them.

Neither Tommy nor Annie had spoken out loud about their desire to have children, or the fact that nothing had happened in that regard as yet. Unbeknownst to each other, they were both beginning to feel concerned that despite their best efforts nothing was occurring.

Tommy had become self-conscious, wondering if the injury he had sustained when he was shot on the front (and which had briefly deprived him of the use of his legs) might have done more damage than he, or his doctors, realised.

Telling himself not to worry about it, and to enjoy these child-free days of his marriage, was not helping either.

Other people were married and within a matter of months were announcing that a new baby was on the way.

Tommy was trying not to make a big deal out of the matter, but he was well aware that Annie would like to have children, and he was troubled that he was failing her. The nagging doubt at the back of his mind, was starting to come between them, mainly because Tommy was worrying so much about it.

If Tommy thought his sister would understand he would have mentioned his worries to her. But Clara seemed indifferent towards having children of her own and had never even mentioned it as a possibility. She might be married now, but she had a career, and she didn't seem to be terribly worried if children happened or they didn't. How could she possibly understand the way he and Annie were feeling?

"Well, I'm going to make a sandwich," Clara remarked, cutting into the silence that had fallen between them. "As Annie isn't here we'll just have to manage by ourselves."

Tommy said nothing.

Clara glanced at her brother as she headed into the pantry, aware of more than he suspected about why he was troubled by his current circumstances. She just had nothing she could say to him that would prevent him from worrying himself unnecessarily. Clara fancied that all things happened in their own time; but equally, sometimes things never happened.

Clara wished she had just the right words of comfort for her brother. In this regard, she found herself lacking. She just had to hope that sooner rather than later there would be good news for Tommy and Annie.

Chapter Twenty-Two

Miss Carter ran a wool shop at the far end of town. Annie couldn't help the smile that came on her face when she spotted the shop's bright array of woollen contents. Annie loved to knit, and she was trying to teach herself to crochet, though the latter handicraft was causing her some difficulty – she didn't quite seem to have the knack.

She would sit and knit for hours and hours, losing track of time as she purled, added and subtracted stitches, and practice all manner of decorative techniques. Her jumpers and scarves were well-regarded in her neighbourhood, and she often made items for the local church fundraising fete.

Yet, Annie had never been to Miss Carter's wool shop simply because it happened to be in the opposite direction to her usual shopping errands and she had been satisfied to use the wool shop that was closer to home.

How she now regretted not having been to Miss Carter's shop before!

Had she only known of the colours, types, thicknesses, and quality of the yarn Miss Carter stocked she would have made the effort to go out of her way and visit this place at least once a month. Annie couldn't help herself as they walked into the shop, and reached out a hand to squeeze a ball of wool and feel how soft it was. A large display of buttons in a cabinet with drawers suddenly caught her eye and immediately diverted her attention. There were so many beautiful buttons! Pretty ones, ones shaped like flowers or animals, practical wooden ones, ones for children and ones for adults. The selection dazzled her, and she had an intense desire to buy at least one of each of the buttons just to have them to hand. Her mind began to spin as she thought about the cardigans she could create to match each unique button.

Gilbert didn't notice Annie's distraction; he was only interested in the task at hand. He waited politely until the only other customer in the shop left and then walked up to Miss Carter with his usual broad smile on his face.

Miss Carter was in her seventies. She had never married, as no man had proven sufficiently interesting to take her away from running her shop. She proudly wore a variety of knitted garments she had made herself, and which she had tailored to elegantly drape her tall, slender physique. She had been a glamorous woman in her youth and that glamour still lingered about her despite her years.

When she was not running her shop, Miss Carter was quite a whiz at designing knitting patterns and regularly submitted these for publication to a number of well-known knitting magazines. Had Annie known, she would probably have discovered that several of the patterns she had knitted were designed by the very lady standing before her.

"Sorry to disturb you," Gilbert raised his hat politely and pulled it to his chest.

Naturally, he was not sorry at all that he had disturbed her, but it was polite to say so.

Annie finally dragged herself away from the display of buttons and joined Gilbert.

"My name is Gilbert McMillan, I am a journalist for the *Brighton Gazette*," Gilbert explained. "This is my assistant Annie Fitzgerald. We are investigating whether there were dubious dealings going on behind the scenes concerning the new bungalows that were built on the clifftop. It has been brought to our attention that certain people who should have known better looked the other way and granted planning permission when they should not have done so. I was told you sold the land to Mr Maguire and were then upset to hear of his plans. Might we talk with you for a bit?"

Gilbert had stated a lot of information in one breath. Miss Carter looked at him slightly aghast. It took her a moment to process what he had just said and regain her composure.

"I would be delighted to tell you my side of this story. Please give me a moment while I shut up the shop."

Miss Carter moved around from the table she used as her counter and went to the door to turn around the sign hanging from it to state she was closed. Then she threw across the lock and motioned for them to follow her through into her backroom.

The back sitting room proved to be another haven for knitted items. Every surface that could take either a doily, a blanket, an anti-macassar or any other sort of knitted item had acquired it. There were even soft toys dotted around including a sweet little cat which Annie picked up and glanced at.

"Why, I do believe I saw this design in a magazine recently. I considered making it, though I don't usually knit toys."

"I designed that little cat," Miss Carter said proudly. "I imagine you are talking about the *Lady's Weekly Magazine*, as that is who I submitted the design to."

"You created the pattern for this cat?" Annie's eyes lit up. "Wait, then you are Little Miss Knitter? I have seen so many of your patterns and always admired them!"

"I am delighted to see that my work has been recognised. The cat has a name, you know. I call him Thomas or Tommy."

Annie squeezed the knitted cat, and a smile came to her face. Tommy the cat. Well, she was just going to have to knit one for herself, wasn't she?

"Tell me again what you are here about," Miss Carter said indicating they should take seats on the sofa. She sat in a tall armchair which held her bolt upright and caused her to look rather like a stern teacher. "I want to know the specifics of why you are asking me questions about that land I sold."

"We are investigating Mr Maguire," Gilbert elaborated. "We have found paperwork that indicates he has been working with people who are prepared to bribe officials to get what they want. We are also aware that he has constructed his bungalows on land that should never have been built on in the first place."

"Mr Maguire is a cheat and a fraud," Miss Carter said, her teeth clamping down hard as if she was imagining biting off his head with a snap. "He bought the land from me cheaply, saying he merely wanted it to use as an allotment garden. If I had known he intended to build upon it, I should never have sold the land to him."

"How did you happen to have the land?" Gilbert asked her.

"It belonged to my late uncle," Miss Carter sighed. "He used to have a cottage not far from the cliffs and the land was part of it. He used it for grazing back in the day, but when he became too old to keep livestock he simply left it to go back to nature. That whole area has always had grazing rights tied to it. Even though it is privately owned, it has been always understood that others could use it for grazing. I think the original clause goes right back to the Norman era.

"After my uncle passed, everything he had I inherited. I had looked after him in his last few years. The cottage I sold to a lovely couple who were just starting out as a family, but they didn't want the extra land. It was simply too much work for them. So I agreed that I would just sell them the cottage and a small piece of land at the back for a garden and the rest I retained. For a long time I didn't think much about the land, it isn't any use to anyone apart from grazing, so I just allowed it to continue to go wild as my uncle had done. Then somehow Mr Maguire learned about the site.

"He came to me one day and asked if I'd be interested in selling the land. I explained to him that the land had very little worth because it could not be used for anything other than grazing. He didn't seem to mind that, and he gave me some story about wanting to start a little allotment there as an extension to the cottage garden business he was already running. I didn't see any reason to doubt what he said and, in all honesty, the money the sale would bring me would be useful. The land was becoming something of a nuisance because it was terribly overgrown and I kept getting complaints from those with gardens neighbouring on to it, saying that it was encouraging rats because no one was managing it.

"Selling the site to Mr Maguire seemed a reasonable way of dealing with the land and avoiding any more problems. I sold it to him for a very nominal sum. Certainly not the amount it was worth if it was going to be used as building land, but then again it *couldn't* be built upon as far as I was concerned. Six months later, I spied a notice in the paper stating that Maguire was looking for planning permission to use that particular patch of land to build five bungalows. I was mortified. The land was *not* to be built upon, it still had the grazing rights attached to it and he had bought it from me cheaply because he said he wasn't going to build upon it! He had cheated me out of money as well as lied to me, so of course I protested."

"You must have been very disheartened when you heard that the planning officers had agreed to his proposal," Annie sympathised with the woman.

"I was fuming," Miss Carter nodded her head. "When I heard what he was doing, I could barely believe it. I made another formal protest to the town hall concerning the fact that the land had traditional grazing rights attached to it and was not to be built upon! But nothing I said did anything. I realised my opinion didn't matter, nor the opinions of anyone who lived near the site or wanted to protest the destruction of an area of common land."

"The reason your protests did nothing is because someone in the planning department had been paid good money to make sure that Maguire got his proposal through," Gilbert told her with a sneaky grin.

Annie wasn't sure he was supposed to be talking about that, but clearly Gilbert thought it was completely appropriate to mention it. Miss Carter looked appalled.

"That is precisely what is wrong with the world today! People choose money over morals, and the rest of us can do nothing about it."

"We're trying to do something about it," Annie told her carefully. "But we need evidence to be sure that Maguire was a willing participant in this scam and not just another innocent dupe."

"An innocent dupe?" Miss Carter laughed. "How could anybody consider that man an innocent dupe? He was the one who came here and bought that land from me! He was the one who smiled in my face and promised me he wasn't going to build upon it. He knew all along what he was up to."

Miss Carter was certainly confirming a few things for them, but her word was not exactly proof. They need something more, something that they could take to the police or, at the very least, something that would shake Maguire enough he would drop the defamation case.

"I imagine there was a sales agreement between you and Mr Maguire?" Gilbert asked.

Miss Carter rose sharply from her seat, surprising them with her sudden movement. She headed to a bureau in the corner of the room and opened a top drawer. Reaching inside, she took out a bundle of papers. She thrust the paperwork at Gilbert.

"I had this agreement drawn up properly by a solicitor, and you will note in one of the clauses there is a written agreement that Mr Maguire would not build upon the land, but I am told by my solicitor that because he went through all the correct routes it would be very difficult to do much about that particular clause. Or rather it would cost me far too much money to take it through the courts. He has deliberately gone against our agreement, but I can do nothing about it because I cannot afford to."

Gilbert took the paperwork and quickly flicked through it. Annie watched him for a moment, feeling her temper rising.

"Mr Maguire is a horrid man," Annie's fists clenched in her lap. "He is hurting my family too. He knows how to use the court system against people, he is double dealing and devious."

"I am sorry he is making you suffer as well," Miss Carter dipped her head at Annie in sorrowful acknowledgement of their shared problem. "I feel stupid about how he fooled me more than anything. I thought the contract would bind him. I thought I could trust a gentleman's agreement."

"This is very serious," Gilbert said, running his finger down a page. "The clause outlines things very clearly. Mr Maguire has gone against this contract, and that means that he has built those houses illegally. Couple that with the fact he also obtained planning permission illegally and it all adds up to some very dodgy business dealings."

Miss Carter was intrigued; she watched silently as Gilbert read through the contract a second time.

"Am I to surmise that there is hope for stopping Mr Maguire and restoring the land to how it should be?" She asked. "Is it possible that you can do something about all this?"

"The more I read from this paper the more certain I am I can do something about it," Gilbert nodded his head. "I don't think it's a matter for the police as such, you want someone who is an expert in contract fraud. Obviously, as a crime has been committed, the police would be involved in arresting Maguire but there are other people who I want to show this to first. Might I be able to take this contract?"

Miss Carter only hesitated for a moment.

"If you think you can finally bring Mr Maguire to justice then of course you can take that contract. I don't like being used and Mr Maguire used me badly. I want to see something done to bring this man crashing back to earth."

Gilbert smiled at her and then folded up the contract to place in his coat pocket.

"In that regard our purposes are aligned, we want to see Maguire brought to justice too."

Miss Carter was mightily relieved, so relieved, in fact, that before she allowed them to leave the shop she insisted Annie pick out some of the buttons she had been admiring earlier.

"And you must take some wool to make up that cat pattern," she added, picking up a ball of light blue wool which she pressed into Annie's hand.

Annie tried to protest, feeling she should not take such gifts from Miss Carter, but the woman would hear none of it.

"You have done me a great service, and I refused to let that go without giving you something as a thank you. I am so glad you came in my shop today. And I don't think I've ever said that about a journalist before, Mr McMillan."

Gilbert merely chuckled.

"I hear that a lot."

"We will do our very best for you," Annie promised the woman.

"You do that," Miss Carter smiled at her. "And when you have used those buttons you must come and show me what you made."

Annie vowed she would endeavour to return soon with good news.

Chapter Twenty-Three

Annie had still not returned home by the time it was drawing close to four. Tommy was becoming increasingly anxious over her absence. Captain O'Harris turned up just before half past three and immediately saw that Tommy was deeply worried.

"What is the matter?" He asked when he saw Tommy staring anxiously out of the window.

"Annie has disappeared," Tommy explained to him.

"Annie has not disappeared," Clara interjected before O'Harris could respond and suggest they organise a search party. "She is clearly on a very important errand. I admit it is unlike her to be absent for dinner, but I have no doubt she has a very good reason. Ask yourselves, why would Annie disappear?"

They had to admit she had a point; Annie was not the sort of person to simply vanish. She wasn't Clara, after all.

The likelihood of Annie getting herself into trouble was extremely slim. Clara was sure that Annie would reappear with a perfectly satisfactory answer for why she had been so late.

Whatever reassuring words Clara said, however, could not prevent her brother from fretting. As Clara glanced at the clock and noted the time she realised there was no chance that she was going to get Tommy to abandon his post by the window.

"Why don't you wait here for Annie and join us later at the pub?" She suggested.

Tommy turned around from the window; his face pulled into an anxious frown.

"I can't leave until I know she is all right, you go on without me."

"I am sure she is fine, old man," O'Harris remarked, trying to sound optimistic. "She'll be home any minute, I imagine."

There was nothing else for it but to leave Tommy to his anxious waiting while they headed off to see if they could finally make some headway in the mystery of the tobacco shop robbery. Neither of them mentioned Annie as they headed out to O'Harris' car, which was parked just outside the house.

Clara had been trying to keep upbeat for her brother, but she was also beginning to be somewhat concerned about Annie's disappearance. She liked to suppose that Annie was sensible enough not to get into any mischief, and surely no one would wish her harm? Yet, sometimes, life did not fall the way you expected it to, and misfortunes happened to the best of people.

They drove to the pub in silence, each deep in their own respective thoughts. The street the pub was situated on was too narrow for the car, so O'Harris parked a couple of roads away and they wandered over to the establishment on foot.

The pub was busier now it was late afternoon. The landlady beamed brightly at Clara when she saw she had returned. She was placing freshly washed pint glasses into a rack just above the bar, from which she could easily access them when she wanted.

"He is in his corner as usual," she told them, nodding with her head in the direction of the bench by the fireplace.

Keats was already nursing a pint as he tried to merge into the shadowy corner.

"I made sure it was watered down again," the landlady winked at them.

Keats glanced up as they approached. He remembered Clara but he didn't know Captain O'Harris.

"I would like to introduce you to my husband Captain O'Harris," Clara began. "I have been telling him about your situation. I hope you don't mind, but John knows a lot about these sorts of things."

Keats glanced in O'Harris' direction. He did not look upset that Clara had spoken about him, more he seemed embarrassed that the handsome and confident Captain O'Harris was suddenly taking an interest in him.

"You need not bother about me, Sir," he said immediately.

"Why do you say that?" O'Harris responded.

"I am a nobody, Sir, just a nuisance to the world at large. I suppose, if I was a braver man I might do away with myself and spare people the bother of me."

"Now that would truly be a crying shame," O'Harris said sincerely. "I suspect you have more to offer the world than you appreciate."

"No, Sir, I am just a problem to everyone. Even when I am trying not to be, I manage to cause people difficulty. Just look at this business with the tobacco shop and my former captain taking responsibility for something I didn't even do. How am I supposed to go through life with people doing things like that for me? I am ruining their lives just by my mere existence."

It was apparent that the situation with the tobacco shop and Joseph Nunn taking the blame on the behalf of Keats had affected the young man deeply. The look of distress upon his face told them all.

"That was not your fault," Clara promised him. "Whomever stole the money and tried to frame you is the one responsible. You cannot take the blame for that upon yourself."

"But if I had not been such a wastrel, then my mother would never have supposed that I could do something like that in the first place," Keats shook his head. "The fact she believed I was capable of such a thing was the reason Joseph took responsibility. I have to accept that there is something about me that makes others suppose I could be a criminal. It hurts one's heart to imagine their own mother believing that they were capable of robbing a shop."

Keats dropped his head forward staring into his pint glass. His sorrow affected them all and made Clara ever more furious with the person responsible for his plight.

"This is why it is so important that we find out who really robbed the shop," Clara said gently.

She wanted to reach out and take his hand but didn't think that would be appropriate. She felt so sorry for him; yet another young man broken by the war, who had been taken advantage of by some immoral scoundrel and believed it was all his own fault.

"We think someone you met here in this pub decided to set you up. They thought you would be easy to blame for the crime."

"They were correct about that," Keats shook his head. "My own mother believes I did it."

"She doesn't believe that now. She should have spoken to you about her concerns before, but I think she has been so worried about you and feared she would make things worse. Many people find it very difficult to help others who are struggling with psychological problems."

"What does that word mean?" Keats asked her.

"Clara is referring to issues of the mind," O'Harris answered on

Clara's behalf. This was his territory, and he was far more experienced at explaining the topic. "Mental problems are not something we're supposed to talk about aloud. It is a crying shame that society at large, and the medical community as a whole, fail to recognise the power of the mind and the dreadful damage that can be done to it by traumatic events such as the war. You are far from alone in suffering from these issues after returning from the war. So many men came home with problems. I would go so far as to argue that the majority who served came home mentally traumatised, and the few exceptions are the ones who we should deem abnormal, rather than normal, in this situation.

"I do all I can to help young men like you who are suffering from the ongoing mental scars inflicted by the war. I run a convalescence home which is for ex-servicemen suffering from all sorts of mental trauma. Damages to the mind need not be physical to cause lasting harm, but it is just as harrowing."

Keats did not know what to make of all this. It was quite apparent that he had never heard about mental trauma and was confused by what they were trying to explain to him.

"The causes of these battles of the mind are complex, but the good news is that it is entirely possible to improve your mental health. I do not go so far as to say my home can fix you completely, but I have helped many men with similar problems to yours, to improve so much they are able to live a regular life again."

"You mean, one where I wouldn't be a bother to everyone?" Keats asked cautiously. "I wouldn't be a nuisance, or a worry?"

"Better than that, I could help you have a life where you are truly alive. Rather than sitting in a room and isolating yourself, you would be back in the world, doing what you should have been doing before the war ever happened. Moving on and creating a future for yourself."

Keats sat and thought about this for a while.

"My mother would like that," he said softly before adding in a mumble. "I would like that."

"Then as soon as this whole matter is resolved, I wish for you to come to the Home. You will not need to stay there as you are so local, but you can come daily, see my doctors, and meet with the other men who we're already helping. I think you will find you have a lot more in common with them than you realise, and it helps to know that there are others going through the same things as you are. Between us all we can begin to unravel the fog and darkness that has wrapped itself around your mind and forced you to close yourself away from the world. All I ask of you is that you make a commitment to coming each day with an open mind."

Keats was looking a little dazed by all this information. After so many years believing he could never be fixed, he had grown bleak about the person he now was. Sometimes he thought about the life he had wanted before the war and regretted all that he had lost, but seeing no way out of his mental quagmire, he simply got on with things and tried not to dwell on the past.

"But first things first," Clara interrupted. "We need you to help us work out who might have tried to frame you for the robbery at the tobacco shop. Is there anyone in this pub who became exceptionally friendly to you around the time of the robbery last year?"

Keats looked blank.

"I don't think anyone here really sees me as a friend," he glanced around him at the people sitting in the pub, not a single one had paid him any attention so far. "I keep myself to myself, that is how I like it. I don't speak to anyone. What is there to talk about after all? I sit here and I watch the world go by. Occasionally the landlady comes over and checks on me, sometimes she'll make me some food, she never asks me to pay for it though I would, you know."

"The landlady is a good woman, looking after you."

"Yes, she watches out for me. I try to help her in return, but there's not a lot I can do. If there is ever any trouble, which is quite rare, then I am always prepared to punch someone's lights out for her. Not that I am much use as a fighter, but I'm always handy as a punching bag."

It was quite obvious that Keats thought extremely little of himself. He had convinced himself that he was a waste of space, that he was of no use to anyone, and this mindset had become deep set. Clara wondered if O'Harris would be able to break through that despair and bring him out of himself, to help him appreciate that there was a place for him in this world, that people cared about him and wanted him to continue to exist in their lives. That Keats had value. O'Harris was looking serious as he listened to Keats, he hadn't said anything for a while, but he wasn't the sort to make assumptions about whether a man could recover or not. In general he liked to believe there was hope for all, but cases like Keats did make him hesitate.

"Just take a look around the pub," Clara said, distracting them both. "Is there anyone here who has spoken to you in the past? Maybe someone who at one point seemed to want to be friends with you, but who then stopped taking an interest?"

Keats obeyed her instruction and glanced around at the faces in the pub. There was now quite a large gathering of people, mainly men who had come in after they had finished work, though a couple of tourists had wandered in to take a look. Once again, Clara was put in mind of people coming to the zoo to gawk at animals, but whether that was how the regular customers perceived things she couldn't say.

Keats shook his head again, sinking into himself a bit further. He was ashamed that he could not give them what they wanted.

"I am sorry, I should be more use to you."

"It does not matter," O'Harris patted his shoulder. "You are doing your best and that is what counts."

Keats looked defeated. Clara was beginning to think they were not helping him with their questions. O'Harris offered to buy him another pint before they left. Keats merely mumbled his thanks but remained looking utterly depressed. Clara feared they had done more harm than good in their efforts trying to help him.

She waited with Keats while O'Harris went and ordered him another pint. The captain returned a moment later and gave it to the young man.

"First thing tomorrow morning, why don't you pop over to my Home?" O'Harris suggested to Keats.

Keats at last looked up and there was a fragile glimmer of hope in his eyes.

"Where is it?"

O'Harris quickly told him the address and then grabbed up a piece of paper from his pocket and drew him out a simple map to show him how to reach the place.

"If you don't turn up, I'll suppose you couldn't find us and I shall come and find you," O'Harris handed the address over to Keats. "How does that sound?"

Keats mumbled his thanks and nodded his head. That was about all they were going to get from him, so they left him in peace to nurse his pint all alone in the corner of the pub. It seemed he was quite right that nobody cared to befriend him or talk to him.

Clara felt sad leaving him alone, but at least they were trying to do something for him, and with any luck he would come to the Home and be able to get some help. In the meantime, they were no further forward in discovering just who had robbed the tobacco shop.

Chapter Twenty-Four

Tommy was very close to calling the police and demanding they begin a search for his wife when he spotted Annie walking along the pavement beside Gilbert McMillan. The rascally journalist was talking to her animatedly, waving his hands around, and Annie was giving him her full attention. Tommy couldn't fathom what was going on and was ashamed to realise that he was feeling a spark of jealousy seeing the pair together. He had no reason to be jealous of Gilbert who was, after all, a rather ugly and disagreeable fellow, yet the thought crossed his mind that he suddenly seemed to be extremely friendly with Annie.

Annie wished Gilbert farewell at the garden gate and walked up to the house door by herself. Tommy positioned himself in the hallway, just in front of the door, so that when she opened it he was the first thing she saw. He had his arms folded across his chest, his earlier worry now turning into anger. He had been fearing the worst for the last few hours and here was Annie just strolling along with Gilbert as if nothing was the matter!

Annie opened the door and stepped into the hallway. She was immediately greeted by Bramble and Pip – dogs not being the sort to hold a grudge about someone being late home. They barged past Tommy in their haste, and he had to put his arm out to stop himself falling over, as a result he lost his stern stance, and Annie assumed his expression of displeasure was due to being nearly knocked over by the dogs.

After greeting the two dogs warmly, she paid closer attention to her husband.

"Did you hurt yourself when the dogs went past you?"

"I am not cross with the dogs, well, not *just* the dogs."

"It is no good standing there scowling at me, Thomas Fitzgerald," Annie said. She had been anticipating such a response from him. "Yes, I am late for dinner, but it is the first time in my life I have ever been so. On the other hand, you and Clara quite regularly miss dinner and rarely offer me an apology. So do not suppose that you can have the upper hand on this one, or permission to act self-righteous."

Annie's remarks had quite taken the wind out of Tommy's sails; he found himself spluttering over the words he had wanted to say.

"Where have you been? I was worried!"

"I had quite a few errands to run," Annie informed him. Then she pulled out the ball of wool she had been given by Miss Carter from her shopping basket along with the buttons. "I discovered a wonderful new wool shop. It is a lot further away than the usual wool shop I go to, but it is so worth the extra effort. Just look at these buttons Tommy! I quite fancy making a cardigan with them."

Before Tommy could say anything else he was having buttons pressed into his hands. He stared at the small wooden objects which had been hand painted with a small floral pattern.

"You have been out all day visiting a wool shop?"

"Of course not, how could anyone spend all day in a wool shop? I have been on several different errands, but that happened to be the last one on my list. The lady who runs it, Miss Carter, is the same person who designs some of the knitting patterns in my favourite magazines!"

Before Tommy could ask another question, Annie began to regale him about the patterns designed by Miss Carter and how wonderful it had been to converse with such a knitting expert. She dug out the magazine containing the pattern for Tommy the Cat, and explained she was going to knit him next and that the wool she was going to use had been picked out by Miss Carter herself.

Tommy began to feel slightly bemused as all this information was directed at him. He also felt a caddish fool. He had worked himself up into such an anguished state, thinking dreadful things had happened to his wife, when all she had been doing was visiting a new wool shop.

Annie seemed like her usual self. As soon as they were back in the kitchen, her hat and coat disposed of, she began preparing dinner which she explained would be a quick fry-up of sausages, chipped potatoes, and some of the eggs from the chickens. It was only then she noticed that her range had gone out.

A hush fell over the kitchen; the dogs sensed that something was amiss and quietly departed to the front room. Tommy knew that if he had any sense, he would depart with them, instead he found himself simply standing there, like a man facing a firing squad, waiting for the explosion that must surely come as Annie stared at the cold coals within her range.

"You let my range go cold?"

Tommy was not going to take the blame for allowing the range fire to die.

"It was cold when we came home," he told his wife. "That was one of the reasons we were so concerned about you. It seemed highly unlikely you would allow the range to go cold if you could help it."

Annie stared instead at the little fire box in the range, which was not giving out even a spark of warmth.

"Well," she said at last, standing up stiffly as if she was doing everything in her power to keep her emotions in check. "I shall just have to relight it, won't I? It is unfortunate, but these things happen, and it is completely fixable."

Her words came out in a staccato fashion which countered her attempt to sound light-hearted about the situation. Tommy sensed that what Annie really wanted to do was rant and rave, but seeing as the only person who she could blame for the range going cold was herself she was restraining her emotion.

Tommy's guilt at being angry over her unexpected absence increased. Seeing how furious Annie was with herself, it didn't seem as though he needed to be angry at her as well. In fact, all he wanted to do now was to console her and tell her she must not be upset with herself. But Annie held herself to a higher standard than everybody else, and she had failed to live up to her own strict rules. Not only was she late for supper but her dereliction of duty had allowed the range to go cold, so their supper would have to be delayed further.

"I should get some coal," Tommy said, edging towards the back door.

"I would've thought you could have considered doing that sooner," Annie said, barely holding on to her temper. "I would have thought you could have looked and seen for yourself that the fire was out and decided to relight the range ahead of my arrival home."

Tommy was not sure what response would save him from a scolding from his wife. Then he remembered that he was not the one who was responsible for the fire going out.

"That is hardly fair. I came home to find you missing and I

have spent hours fretting about you and wondering if I should start searching the streets."

"Why would you need to start searching for me?" Annie snapped.

"I thought you might have come to some harm!" Tommy snapped back. "Now I wonder why I was even concerned! Why should I worry about someone who storms back in after being missing for two days, leaving me worried sick, and immediately starts to badger me about letting the range go cold!"

"I have hardly been *missing* for two days," Annie retorted. "I have been here in the evenings. I made you breakfast this morning."

"I don't know what is going on with you Annie, and if you want to talk about it then I will certainly listen. But don't start bullying me or making me your whipping boy for things going wrong in your kitchen that were the result of your absence. I am starting to wonder why I wasted my afternoon worrying about you!"

"You do not know the half of what I have been doing," Annie threw back at him. "I have not been out of the house all this time simply for my own pleasure, you know!"

"Then what have you been doing? For that matter, why are you suddenly chummy with Gilbert McMillan? I thought you despised the fellow."

"I may have misjudged him in the past," Annie shook her head at her husband. "If you only knew what I have been trying to do."

"The only way I can know what you have been trying to do is if you actually tell me about it!" Tommy shouted; it was unusual for him to raise his voice and certainly he never raised his voice at Annie, but his emotions were getting the better of him.

It wasn't just that he had been worried about Annie's absence, there were other things on his mind, like his secret worry that he was somehow failing his wife. That worry had been gnawing at him, churning up his insides and bringing out a side of him he did not much care for.

Now, here was Annie keeping secrets from him, when in the past she had always confided in him.

"What is happening between us, why will you no longer talk to me?"

Annie spun around and glanced at him in surprise.

"I talk to you all the time. I am talking to you right now."

"You know exactly what I mean. You are up to something that you are keeping close to your heart, and it clearly does not involve me, but it does involve Gilbert McMillan."

Annie just stared at him, astonished by the sudden venom in his words.

"You are surely not jealous of Gilbert McMillan?"

"I am not sure what to think anymore, or what to feel," Tommy answered, his words bitter. "I keep thinking I've done something wrong, that I have let you down somehow, and then all I can think to myself is how I try so hard Annie, and yet still you go off in secret as if you can't trust me! I spent all afternoon worrying where you were, and the first thing you do is come in and shout at me for letting the range go cold. How is that supposed to make me feel?"

The words hung heavy in the air. Tommy was not usually so forthright. Annie took a deep breath before she spoke, aware that if she allowed her tongue to get away from her she could easily say something she would regret.

"You are right, I shouldn't have tried to blame you for the range. I am to blame, and I don't like being at fault."

Tommy was taken aback by what was in essence an apology. Annie's contrition made him even more alarmed – she did not normally back down or admit to making a mistake.

"Are you going to tell me what this is all about?" He demanded.

Annie placed her hands on her hips, for a second she looked fearsome, as if she might deny everything and tell him he was being a fool. Then her eyes softened, and she walked towards Tommy. He realised she was going to hug him, and his anger made him almost step back, then he checked himself. Annie was not often physically demonstrative about her affection for him, turning her away would be churlish. It took him a moment to accept her embrace as she slipped her arms around him, but he did eventually link his own arms around her and clasp her tightly to him.

It was in that instant he remembered why he loved Annie and why he could never be angry at her for long. He was also reminded why he had been so worried in the first place. The fear of losing her was the worst thing he had ever felt. He had been jealous of Gilbert for the irrational reason that he was scared that one day Annie might decide she didn't need him anymore.

"I would have spoken to you sooner about what I was up to, but I feared you would be angry. I hoped to have everything all arranged before I had to tell you."

Tommy was anxious about this statement.

"Why? What have you been up to?"

"I made a decision to deal with Mr Maguire for you and Clara," Annie pulled back from her husband so she could look up into his face. "That ghastly man has caused you and Clara such grief for no reason, and I decided it was my turn to take care of you two. You have been so brave about it all, saying you will just go to a solicitor and fight his claims. I decided I needed to do something to put a stop to this business before it went too far. What I have been up to might be considered morally dubious, but the results are more than I could have imagined and justify the means."

"Now I am very curious as to what you've been up to," Tommy said, raising an eyebrow and wondering just what his wife had gotten herself into.

"I have done nothing dreadful," Annie began. "I have been investigating Mr Maguire with the assistance of Gilbert McMillan. My goal was to determine if there was something about him, something illegal, that you could use against him. Since a stern talking to had not deterred him from his course of action, I thought he might need some greater persuasion to drop the defamation case."

"Wait a minute, are you saying you went and confronted Mr Maguire?"

Annie smiled proudly; she was delighted to see how amazed Tommy was that she had done such a thing.

"I did go and have a word with him, but it did absolutely no good. That man is completely reprehensible! I decided I would have to go about things in a different way, which is why I asked Gilbert to help me. Together we have been digging into Mr Maguire's private affairs and we have at last found something that proves he is a scam artist. We are now trying to decide what to do with this information."

"Annie, are you saying you have been gathering information so you could blackmail Mr Maguire into dropping the defamation case?"

"Blackmail is a nasty word, Tommy, and I won't hear it," Annie wagged a finger at him. "I have only been determining just what sort of a man Mr Maguire is, and if there is some way I could convince him it would be in his best interest to stop harassing you and Clara. As it happens, what I have discovered is far bigger than what I had anticipated."

Tommy could hardly believe what he was hearing. Never in his wildest dreams had he imagined his wife would be up to something like this – investigating a man to prove that he was a scoundrel? She was starting to sound altogether too much like Clara.

"And what have you found?" He asked, fascinated by this turn of events despite his unease.

"We have learned that Mr Maguire bought the piece of land along the cliffs under false pretences from a lady who wouldn't have sold it to him if she knew he was going to build on it. We know that, through a friend, he had a planning officer bribed into granting planning permission. We know he had a surveyor's reports to state that the land was unsuitable for building work, and yet he built the houses anyway. In short, through nefarious means Mr Maguire has created these bungalows which he intends to sell quickly and then disappear before anybody realises that they're living in something that's going to crumble away into the sea in a few years' time."

"That is certainly unexpected," Tommy said in amazement.

"It is more than unexpected. It is the means for us to end this nightmare. Mr Maguire wants to destroy your reputations as detectives out of vengeance. Now I have found all this information about him, we can stop him. Whether we do that through the police or simply by persuading Maguire to dismiss the defamation case, the outcome will be the same. You and Clara no longer have to worry about Mr Maguire and his efforts to take you to court. Mr Maguire has every reason to be worried about *me*. He will rue the day that he laughed at me on his doorstep and told me I could do nothing about what he was doing."

Tommy had never seen this side of Annie before, but her determination and her delight that she had managed to find this information out about Mr Maguire was undeniable. He was seeing her in a whole new light. He was not sure if he was excited by this new Annie, or slightly disturbed.

Chapter Twenty-Five

They sat in O'Harris' car to contemplate what they were going to do next. Clara was not sure how they could determine who had truly robbed the tobacco shop when they didn't have anybody on their suspect list. The fact that Keats could not remember anybody being exceptionally friendly to him prior to the robbery was no help at all. They were lacking information or any clue as to what had really occurred.

While his wife was contemplating how she could discover who had really stolen the tobacco shop money, O'Harris was wondering how he could help Keats and just what it might take to bring him back to living a normal life.

How had he missed that a man in his own town was suffering so badly from the traumas of war?

The thought nagged at him, bringing with it a sensation of guilt that he had failed Keats. Who knew how many other men just like Keats were living in Brighton ignored and forgotten? Wasn't he failing them too?

Clara was growing cold as they both sat in their respective thoughtful gloom. She was about to suggest they ought to head home, glancing out the window towards the pub as she did so. It was at that moment her attention was drawn to a man walking along the path. Though he had his coat collar pulled up and his hat was down over his ears Clara was sure she recognised him. The words she had been about to say died on her lips as she watched the man entering the building and realised who he was.

"Stuart Greaves just went into the pub!"

O'Harris glanced in the direction she had been looking, seeing only a disappearing figure as the man made his way through the door. He turned back to his wife and met her keen gaze.

"That is quite the coincidence, isn't it?"

"Coincidence, my foot! We are quite some distance from the tobacco shop and there are plenty of pubs nearer to it that Stuart could frequent."

Both O'Harris and Clara were now looking across the street at the pub.

"I need to know what he is doing," Clara made up her mind. "But we will both be recognised immediately if we now enter the pub. We have no idea if Stuart is working alone or if he has a complicit friend he is now meeting. If his companion saw us talking to Keats earlier, he may warn Stuart, and he will avoid us."

"Then we need to be cunning," O'Harris replied. "Maybe we can see through the window and spy on Stuart?"

Clara pulled a face, feeling that this was too risky.

Yet there seemed no other way to learn what Stuart might be doing inside the pub. Reluctantly, she agreed to the idea, and they abandoned the negligible warmth of the car. The pub windows were only partly masked by shutters so they could glance through and easily spy on Stuart while remaining largely out of sight. Stuart was at the bar talking to the landlady. He seemed to be in an animated conversation with her, a moment later she was handing him a pint with a smile and laughing in his direction.

"He seems to be in there alone," O'Harris remarked to his wife. "If he is here to meet someone they have not arrived yet."

They watched him for a while longer, but Stuart just sat at the bar sipping his pint and occasionally saying something to the landlady as she went past.

"This is no good, I have to get inside there and see what he is doing," Clara grumbled. "This cannot simply be a coincidence. He is here for a reason, and I want to know what that reason is."

"This all supposes that Stuart was somehow involved in the crime," O'Harris reminded her. "What if he wasn't?"

"I admit I have no real reason to suspect Stuart of the robbery," Clara pulled a face. "But here we have him at the pub, a place I wasn't expecting to see him, and we have a connection at last between the tobacco shop and Keats."

Clara was itching to get back inside the pub, but she knew that would prove fruitless. They crossed back over to the car to consider their next move.

"Stuart must be involved somehow," Clara shook her head. "I ought to have realised it sooner."

"You said there was no evidence or a motive for him being behind the robbery," O'Harris replied.

"None that I know of, but that hardly means Stuart is innocent. I just haven't found the right piece of the puzzle yet."

Clara was close to storming into the pub and demanding Stuart told them what he was up to, when Keats stumbled out of the building, looking more miserable than ever. It appeared that he had

had enough of nursing his pint for the evening and was about to head home.

Clara glanced at O'Harris, then immediately hopped across the road to grab Keats' arm. He was too bemused by the gesture to resist as she pulled him back to where O'Harris was stood wondering what she was up to.

"Stuart Greaves has just walked into the pub," Clara explained to Keats, her voice urgent. "We want to know why he is here all of a sudden, but we cannot go in and just ask him. He would not tell us. We need you to go inside and speak to him for us."

"I think what my wife meant to say was, 'would you be prepared to go back inside and find out why Stuart has suddenly arrived here?'" O'Harris gently readjusted the question so it sounded less like a command.

Keats had that dazed look on his face again and seemed unsure of what they were saying, then something they had said must have finally filtered through to his mind and a memory sparked there.

"I don't need to go back into the pub to tell you why Stuart Greaves is there," Keats waved his hand at the building. "Stuart comes here regularly to visit the landlady."

And just like that a piece of the puzzle had fallen into place.

The connection between the tobacco shop, the pub, and Keats.

"Would the landlady be his girlfriend?" Clara asked.

"I suppose you could say that," Keats nodded his head. "They have been seeing each other for well over a year now. He pops in most afternoons to see her. He is rather late today, he's usually here before me."

Clara knew why Stuart had not been there earlier; he had been avoiding the place until they had left. The landlady must have warned him to stay away as they had been asking questions and were returning.

After they had left, she had somehow signalled to Stuart that he could finally make an appearance. She was not to know that Clara and O'Harris had a car outside they had been sitting in. She would have presumed they had gone home.

"Does Stuart ever talk to you, Keats?"

"Never," Keats replied. "He knows who I am, I suppose. He probably remembers me from the time I worked in the tobacco shop before the war as a delivery boy. But he keeps away from me."

They had the link at last, but that didn't explain to them the motive. If Stuart had stolen the money from the tobacco shop what was his reason for doing so? Without a motive, all they had was some extremely flimsy circumstantial evidence.

"Do you need me to go back inside now?" Keats asked them. "It's rather cold out here, if you don't need me to go back in the pub, I think I'll go home."

Clara agreed that he had already done more than enough to aid them, and that he should go home. After he had left to wend his way back to his solitary rooms, she found herself feeling deeply confused about Stuart's involvement in the case. As she returned once more to the car with O'Harris, she aired some of her thoughts to try to make sense of them.

"If Stuart and the landlady's relationship is the reason they chose Keats to plant the money on, she did a good impression of being shocked by the matter and being upset that Keats had been used. I don't like people who can be so two-faced."

"Unless she knows nothing about what Stuart did?" O'Harris postulated. "I wonder what happened that required Stuart to suddenly need the money,"

"Debt is always a possibility. Though Stuart gets an allowance from his mother he could easily be spending beyond his means. If he is in debt, then maybe we can figure out who he is in debt to, and that will at last give us the link. Or maybe he stole the money for his landlady friend? There was me thinking she really did care about Keats and was treating him in a motherly fashion. I hate to think that she lied to me and was actually using him."

"People do some terrible things when it comes to money," O'Harris sighed. "But you are a step closer to figuring this all out, Clara, and that is what matters. For now though, why don't we get out of the cold and get back home. Our dinner is no doubt calling to us, and there will be plenty of time to take this further tomorrow."

Clara concurred that it was time to call it a day. They couldn't barge into the pub and start asking questions with Stuart present. They needed to wait until their two suspects were alone and interrogate them separately. Only that way would they be able to finally determine what was going on.

Annie and Tommy had a long discussion about what she had discovered concerning Mr Maguire. Tommy was impressed at how deeply Annie had managed to dig into Maguire's past, and the secrets that she had unearthed. The real problem was what they were going to do with this information.

"Gilbert thinks we might at last have enough to push for Maguire to be found guilty of fraud. He says he knows someone he can show the paperwork to, and they can give him a professional opinion about whether there is enough to make a case against Maguire, and then we can go to the police," Annie explained.

"What you have achieved Annie is extraordinary," Tommy responded, still not quite able to believe that their problems with Maguire might be at an end. "I don't think Clara could have done a better job. You have really gone above and beyond for the both of us. I feel awful now for being so angry about your absence. I should have had greater faith in you."

Annie simply shook her head.

"Secrets always bring out the worst in people," she said kindly. "In hindsight, I should have spoken to you sooner, but I wanted to have all my information in place before I raised your hopes. I didn't want you to think I was interfering. I know you and Clara wanted to sort this out yourselves. I just felt it needed a different approach, it needed someone who was prepared to look at things from another angle and perhaps to not behave in quite as upstanding a manner as you and Clara usually do."

"I don't know where you got the idea that Clara and I ever tried to be upstanding," Tommy chuckled. "I think you have been amazing Annie. I don't know how to ever say how grateful I am to you."

"You don't have to be grateful. People do these sorts of things for their loved ones without question and without expectation of reward or thanks. It's what being family means, or at least it's what it means to me."

Annie reached out and clasped his hand, she smiled at him warmly. Tommy felt closer to her than he had done in a while; he realised now that all his worries about them having a baby had begun to put a block between him and his wife. One that was completely unnecessary. He had been trying too hard, trying to anticipate what would please Annie and, as a result, he had ended up drifting away from her.

"I am proud of you Annie," he said. "But there is something else. This whole thing has made me realised that we mustn't have secrets from each other. We have always been honest with each other in the past, and that should never change. You should never feel you cannot come to me and tell me something."

"That goes for you as well," Annie replied. "You and Clara can always speak to me, and I will listen to whatever you have to say. Sometimes I will think you are doing something that is foolish, but at the same time I still want to know what you are up to and what worries you. We are a team, aren't we? And as a team we should always be prepared to speak to each other and tell each other what is troubling us, or what makes us happy."

Tommy felt a spasm of discomfort at this statement. There was something that was strongly on his mind.

"In this new situation of complete honesty, there is something I want to mention. I have been feeling very…"

Tommy tapped his finger on the table, he was unsure how to complete that sentence, but he knew he had to.

"I have been worrying that I cannot give you what you desire the most. It has been on my mind that when I was injured at the front, I perhaps sustained a secondary injury that no one knew about," Tommy took a deep breath, the words coming hard as he fought with his pride and shame. "I have been considering going to a doctor, to see if there is a reason why I haven't been able to give you a baby. I should have spoken about it sooner. I feel terrible that I am failing you as a husband."

Tommy dropped his gaze from Annie's eyes. Speaking aloud his fears had been difficult, but there was a sense of relief now they were out. All that remained, was the dread as he waited for Annie's response.

"You are not failing me, Tommy."

"You're being too generous, I know you want to have children, and

I want to be able to give them to you. I feel so bad that something might be wrong with me that I cannot do that."

"Tommy you are not failing me," Annie repeated insistently.

"You don't have to try and make me feel better."

"No, Tommy, you are not *listening* to me," Annie said to him firmly. "You have *not* failed me."

She repeated the words, carefully emphasising each one, then she took his hand and placed it on her belly.

"I am not trying to make you feel better, I am telling you the truth."

Tommy stared at her for a moment unable to think what to say.

"You mean, you are…?"

Annie nodded her head at him. Tommy's words dried up, he couldn't think of anything else to say, instead, he simply leaned forward and embraced her in a hug.

"You could have told me sooner."

"I wanted to be sure. Had I known you were worrying so, I would have told you before."

Tommy simply chuckled into her ear.

"I'm not as broken as I feared then."

"You are not broken at all Tommy. You are perfect to me."

"Even if I did fail to relight the range when I realised it was out?"

Annie huffed.

"All right, maybe not perfect, but you do try hard."

Chapter Twenty-Six

The following day Clara returned to her old house and met up with Tommy to explain what she had discovered. She was relieved to see that Annie was happily bustling about in the kitchen making tea and breakfast for everyone. The dogs were watching her with rapt attention, certain she was bound to share something with them to make up for her absence over the last few days.

Tommy could not wait to reveal all the news he had to tell Clara. He motioned her into the dining room where, on the table, was a list he had made of all the information Annie had gathered about Maguire. Clara glanced through it, her eyes widening as she realised just what Annie had been up to and how successful her investigations had been.

"Annie did this all by herself?"

"She had the help of Gilbert McMillan."

Clara was even more amazed to learn that her sister-in-law had been prepared to work with the journalist on this matter.

"There is enough here to completely ruin Mr Maguire, it is obvious that he has been committing a fraud not just against the people who he was selling the properties to but against the general public by his attempts to manipulate the system we have in place for planning permission."

"What do you want to do with this information?" Tommy asked her carefully. "We could merely show it to Maguire and have him drop the defamation case, or we could do something more."

"I am surprised you even have to ask," Clara said to him. "Quite obviously we're going to take this to the police and have them deal with the matter. Maguire will have to drop the defamation case when all this comes out. He is going to have enough difficulty defending himself in this affair. I am not sure what the legal punishment is for something like this, but I could imagine him ending up doing some time in prison."

"Mr Mullins got away lightly it seems, by his convenient heart attack."

"I am not sure he would see it that way. But his heart attack has been useful for us, enabling us to find these documents which otherwise we never would have been able to get hold of. Annie has been truly remarkable."

"You aren't the only one who investigates mysteries," Annie was in the doorway of the dining room with a tray of tea things. She was feeling proud as punch to hear Clara praise her efforts so heartily. "I am glad to hear that you are going to follow the proper process with all this. There was a point when I would have considered blackmailing Mr Maguire if it had achieved my purpose, but I much prefer it this way."

Clara turned and gave Annie a hug. The smaller woman stiffened in her embrace, taken by surprise at the gesture.

"I cannot tell you how thankful I am for this Annie. What you have done for us, I cannot put into words. You have really saved us."

Annie was humbled by this statement, and also somewhat embarrassed, she was not keen on praise unless it was in relation to her cooking. She pulled away from Clara and set about pouring out tea.

"With all that sorted, the only thing we have left to look at is this matter of the tobacco shop robbery," Tommy reminded them. "Clara, before I distracted you with all this business concerning Mr Maguire, you were saying something about having new information about the robbery?"

"Stuart Greaves is very friendly with the landlady of the pub where Keats regularly drinks," Clara explained. "My understanding is that they are in a relationship, which means that she must be the 'girlfriend' he said he was with at the time of the robbery. That is our link between the tobacco shop and Keats, but I haven't got any further than that. If Stuart was responsible for the robbery, and unfortunately I have no proof of that, then it would make sense that when things became complicated he found a way to deposit some of the money on Keats to shift the blame. The problem is supposition alone will not clear Joseph Nunn's name."

Tommy frowned as he took stock of what Clara was saying.

"What we really need is to discover what happened to the money that was stolen which was not passed to Keats. We know that around £25 was in that safe at the time of the robbery. £15 of that money was given to Keats in an effort to frame him, but what happened to the other £10? Stuart must have intended to keep the lot originally, and it was a sizeable amount which means he must have needed a considerable sum of money in a hurry. Was he in debt perhaps? Or was there something he wished to purchase?"

Tommy was idly glancing at his wife as he aired his thoughts, watching her hands move over the tea things. At that moment he glimpsed the engagement ring on her finger and a thought struck him.

"Stuart Greaves gets an allowance from his mother, that allowance must cover all his usual expenses but perhaps it isn't enough for extra items, the sort of extra expensive items that come up only once in a lifetime?"

Clara waited for him to elaborate on this thought.

"The landlady at the pub, do you remember her hands when she was serving us?" Tommy watched his sister's face as she frowned and shook her head. "I noticed in that absent minded way you do sometimes, that she had an engagement ring on her finger. The reason I noticed was because it clattered against the side of my pint glass as she served me. I didn't think anything of it at the time because the woman had mentioned she had been married, so naturally she would have had an engagement ring. But now it occurs to me that she was *only* wearing an engagement ring. There was no wedding band!"

"Are you sure?" Clara asked, knowing this could be significant if her brother was correct.

Tommy chewed on his lower lip.

"Fairly sure. I mean, I wasn't really paying attention at the time, but I am almost certain her wedding band was missing."

"Wedding rings get lost," Annie pointed out. "Hands get bigger and sometimes rings have to be removed as they become too tight. A widow without a wedding ring could mean a lot of things."

"But it could mean she has become re-engaged to someone else. Thus the engagement ring Tommy glimpsed was not the one given to her by her late husband but by a new admirer," Clara could see where Tommy was going with this. "You think that the landlady got that ring from Stuart. That he stole the money from the safe to purchase it."

"It is quite obvious that Stuart Greaves has never worked a day in his life and never intends to, my assumption is that he likes to be taken care of, and with his mother ageing, he has finally decided to find a wife to essentially replace her. The landlady at the *Mallard* is both amenable, motherly and has a source of income that could provide for a layabout husband – not that she probably is aware of how lazy her prospective spouse is. She will suit Stuart to the ground.

"But an engagement ring is pricey, and I can't imagine Stuart being very good at saving up his own allowance to purchase one. He would have looked for an easier option, and he knew that in his mother's safe there was a big sum of money that would allow him to purchase an extravagant engagement ring, one that would certainly delight the landlady and convince her that she had a man of means courting her.

"We shall have to surmise that Stuart didn't want his mother knowing what he was up to. Perhaps he knew she wouldn't approve of him becoming associated with a woman considerably older than him. Whatever the case, he stole the money to buy the engagement ring, thinking that his mother would just accept the robbery as one of those things, or that the police would not be terribly interested in the whole affair. But matters became out of hand, his mother wouldn't just accept what had happened, she passed onto the police a list of suspects. Suddenly, Stuart feared he might be held accountable for the crime when the police failed to find a culprit, and so he gave a sizeable amount of the money to Keats in secret, so that when the police went to investigate him, they would discover he suddenly had money and would imagine he was responsible.

"It meant buying a cheaper ring for his lady love, but that was the price for his freedom. Then, of course, the situation became complicated when Joseph Nunn decided to step in and take the blame for Keats. That didn't particularly worry Stuart, though. After all, if the man was prepared to take the fall for his crime why should he worry about it? After that things played out as we all know."

"It is a good supposition and an interesting theory," Clara said.

"But how do we prove that is what really happened? We have no proof Stuart took that money."

"We have to find where he bought the ring from."

Tommy moved across the room and picked up a book from the shelf which proved to be their well-thumbed street directory. He began to flick through it quickly.

"I'm going to say that Stuart Greaves' inherent laziness means it is very unlikely he went to great lengths to find a jeweller to purchase the ring from. My thinking is, he bought it from the first shop he found, so I am going to look for the nearest jewellers to the tobacco shop."

Tommy ran his finger down a page, and it was not long before he came across the information he wanted. Two streets along from the tobacco shop there was a jewellery shop. It was old and well-established and had paid for a full-page advert in the directory. If they had money to splash out on publicity like that, Tommy imagined their products were pricey.

"This is where we go to find out the solution to this mystery," Tommy jabbed his finger at the page.

"I'm impressed," Clara said. "You two carry on this way, I don't think you'll even need me anymore. I shall just have to go and be a housewife."

Tommy knew she was joking; Annie however was appalled at the thought of her role being reversed with Clara's.

"You will do no such thing," she said instantly. "You are the detective here and never forget it, just because you've been a little bit distracted since you were married doesn't change anything. Now both of you get out there and solve this mystery, you are under my feet, and I have a lot of work to do today to make right the neglect caused by my absence. This house has quite gone to the dogs while I was busy."

Clara and Tommy both glanced around the room, trying to fathom what Annie could possibly mean by the house 'going to the dogs' in just the two days she was gone. Possibly, if they looked hard enough, there might be a speck of dust here and there, and the floor hadn't been swept, but to suggest the house was in a state of shambles from Annie's neglect was to go too far. However, Annie would not hear any talk about the house being perfectly acceptable. She was convinced that she had disgracefully abandoned her duties and was more than happy to get back to work.

There was nothing that pleased Annie more than getting the house in order. A person could truly relax when they were sweeping or dusting. The weight of the world would lift from your shoulders, and you didn't have to worry about a thing.

Annie thought people didn't appreciate just how soothing housework was, and she fancied that a lot of people would be better off if they spent more time *doing* housework and less time *worrying*.

Leaving her to attack the house and clean it from top to bottom, Tommy and Clara headed off to the jewellers they had discovered in the street directory. They didn't have any trouble finding it, as it was the most prominent shop in the road.

The premises had a frontage which was double that of any of the other shops in the row, with large bay windows either side of a door. The woodwork was painted a deep bottle green and gold lettering both above the windows and on their glass informed passersby that the establishment had been sitting there selling all manner of fine jewels since 1867.

In the well-lit windows were shelves upon shelves of jewellery displayed on black velvet-covered stands, gold and silver sparkling in the daylight. Clara noted that the windows were reinforced by thin bars that ran across them just in case a thief decided to try their luck. There was also a metal folding shutter behind the windows that would be pulled across and locked at night to act as another security measure.

When Clara looked at the price tags on some of the jewels in the window she could see why the proprietors of the business were being so cautious.

They headed inside and walked to the nearest counter (the shop having two, set opposite one another). The counter they had chosen due to its proximity to the door also happened to hold a display of fine rings, the prices listed beside them making Clara goggle.

She hoped O'Harris had not spent such a sum on her engagement and wedding rings. It would make her feel quite nervous to be walking around with such high-priced items on her finger.

On their way to the shop, Clara and Tommy had devised a plan to gather the information they needed. Tommy now took the lead and smiled broadly at the older gentleman stood behind the counter.

"I do hope you can help me," Tommy began. "I am here to buy an engagement ring. My sister said this was the best shop to buy one from."

He motioned to Clara as he spoke.

"And my friend Stuart Greaves tells me he just bought a ring from you. I have seen the ring he bought, and I would like to have one as similar to it as possible, though not identical, of course, that would be unseemly. The lady friend I am about to propose to has also seen that particular ring and has admired it so I know she will appreciate one similar to it."

Putting on his best charming smile and attempting to sound a little nervous as well as baffled by this ring business, Tommy thought he played the part of an aspiring husband pretty well.

"I am afraid I shall need more details than what you have supplied to determine the ring your friend purchased," the jeweller said, picking up a ledger sitting to his left.

"Oh, of course. He purchased the item at the end of the summer," Tommy added. "I should say around the end of July."

The jeweller turned his ledger pages back to the previous year.

"The name was Greaves?" He asked, running a finger down a page.

"Yes, Stuart Greaves," Tommy said keenly.

"I have the entry here. He purchased an engagement ring on the 1st of August and brought it back a week later to be resized," the jeweller tapped his finger on the handwritten entry. "He purchased a ring with a style of diamond we call a princess cut. The ring was made of 9 carat gold, one of our more affordable items. This particular ring had a further discount on the price as it was old stock, and I was making room for new items. Unfortunately, I do not have anything similar to that ring's design at this time, but I could show you other rings of comparable quality."

Tommy attempted to appear disappointed.

"That's a pity, I don't suppose you could tell me how much it was? I have in mind a budget, but it always helps to know what I should expect to spend."

"Why yes, the ring was £10 exactly, though that does not include the price of sizing it."

Tommy glanced at his sister, the smile increasing on his face. She smiled back.

"Thank you, that is exactly what we needed to know."

Chapter Twenty-Seven

They were closer to the truth, but there were still elements missing. After a quick consultation outside the jewellery shop, Clara and Tommy agreed that they would speak once again to those involved. They wanted to discuss what they had discovered with Joseph Nunn and Keats. Between the four of them, they hoped they might think of a way to resolve this matter.

Keats was the easiest person to find as he was the nearest, so they went to his flat first. Unsurprisingly, the young man was in his room, though he looked slightly abashed when they found him only half dressed. He had clearly not been awake very long.

"I don't really get visitors other than my mother," Keats apologised for his appearance. "Are you checking that I am going to go see Captain O'Harris today? I will go, I swear to it, but maybe a little bit later, when I have had time to get myself organised."

Clara suspected that Keats had no intention of going to the convalescence home, but that was not what she was there for.

"We need you to come with us when we now go to speak to Joseph

Nunn. We think we know who really robbed the tobacco shop, but we want to speak to you both to air out our theory and decide on a way to move forward with this."

Keats looked uneasy about leaving his flat, there was a moment when he looked like he was going to protest. Clara reached out and caught his arm.

"You have to come, this isn't just about you anymore, this is about helping Joseph. You said yesterday that you felt awful about what had happened, about people taking the blame for you. Well, that is why you need to come with me right now, to make amends for what happened. It is time you stopped hiding away in these rooms and saw the world for what it is again."

Keats looked like he might refuse, but then his expression changed as he realised what she was saying.

"You are right, I have been spending all my time hiding away. And I do owe Joseph a lot. I shall come with you. I shall do what I can."

They were both relieved to hear this.

After Keats had dressed and made himself look as presentable as was possible in his unwashed, crumpled clothes, they made their way to Joseph Nunn's own set of small rooms. Keats told them as they travelled that he had never been to Joseph's home. Joseph had always come to his property, or his mother's, so he had never seen where his former captain lived.

Clara wondered just what Keats would make of seeing the man he admired so much living in almost as bad a shambles as he was. She fancied that Joseph and Keats had far more in common than either of them realised and, before this day was done, she was going to make sure that both of them went to O'Harris' convalescent home and started their journeys to recovery. That was the least she could do for them, after she had cleared Joseph's name.

They found Joseph at home. He was surprised to see Keats on his doorstep, but when he saw that Clara and Tommy were there too he realised what was going on.

"You found something out," he said, trying to hide his enthusiasm.

"We certainly have," Tommy replied. "The question we have now is what we're going to do with the information we have discovered."

Joseph welcomed them into his room, and they found places to sit as best they could. Clara and Tommy once again perched on the bed, while Keats accepted the chair that Joseph offered him. Joseph leaned against the wall, his hands in his pockets, ready to listen to all they said.

Clara slowly outlined what they had discovered so far; as she repeated their theory, she realised it didn't amount to much without proof. She wasn't the sort of person to beat herself up about a failure, but in that moment, she found herself feeling guilty she could not offer the pair greater hope.

When they were finished, Joseph just stood with his mouth open, looking amazed at what they were saying, while Keats was clenching his fists in his lap.

"I cannot believe I was so wrong about Stuart," Joseph said. "I thought he had no reason to be considered a suspect."

"The way Stuart conducts his life, he certainly makes it seem as though he would have no reason to steal anything," Tommy agreed. "However, what we have discovered tells us otherwise."

"To think he was at the pub all this time, watching me and planning what he was going to do," Keats said barely holding on to his fury at the revelation.

"I don't think Stuart intended for you to take the blame initially," Clara tried to gently soothe his temper. "The idea came to him afterwards, when he realised the police were not going to let things rest. He became desperate to deflect the blame from himself while also wanting to retain some of the money he had stolen. He still wanted to buy a ring for his lady love. He decided to give you the bulk of the stolen money, enough to attract suspicion to you, while making it appear you had spent some already. He was hoping the police wouldn't look too hard for the remainder, which is exactly what happened."

"And then I came along, spoke to Mrs Keats, and jumped to completely the wrong conclusion," Joseph shook his head thinking how foolish he had been, how he had made assumptions based on his own misinformation and ended up suffering needlessly as a consequence. "I took the blame just like that! Stuart must have thought it was his lucky day. The police had been looking at me as their prime suspect right from the start, and I just made it easy for them after that."

"Stuart owes us both a great deal," Keats said angrily.

It was the first time they had seen him so animated; On all their prior visits he had seemed dulled and disheartened by life, nothing stirring him up to feel emotional. There had seemed a wall inside Keats, preventing him from feeling or expression emotions. Now that wall had dropped, and his temper was revealed. He suddenly looked alive.

"The problem we have is how we prove Stuart did this," Clara told them. "I can't see the evidence we currently have exactly encouraging the police to open this case again, especially when they've already successfully arrested and had one man convicted of the crime. It will take more than the purchase of an engagement ring to convince the police to look into this matter further and overturn your conviction, Joseph. Which is why we came to you two. We hope by having a discussion we will come up with an idea of where to go next with this situation."

"What are you thinking we should do?" Joseph asked.

"The main problem I see is that without some conclusive evidence nothing will change, but if Stuart could be persuaded to confess to what he did, then that is another matter," Clara explained. "How we persuade him is the tricky part. I am not one to encourage brute force when other methods are available to us, but with the length of time since the original crime and the lack of any clues we have linking Stuart to the robbery, I think it's important that we consider all our options."

Joseph glanced towards Keats. Keats was frowning, not quite sure what Clara was saying.

"I am telling you two that I think it would be worthwhile if you confronted Stuart. Tell him you know what he did, that you worked it out for yourselves," Clara looked to Keats. "Maybe, Keats, you might mention that your landlord remembers who dropped off that envelope he passed on to you."

"That would be a lie," Keats looked uncomfortable. "The envelope was posted through the front door and my landlord found it on the mat."

"Then you tell Stuart that he was seen out of a window posting the envelope," Clara impressed upon him. "We have to take a chance and assume he delivered the item in person. You just need to convince him that you know he is responsible for the robbery and the envelope of money, and that you will go to the police unless he goes to them first and confesses."

"It won't be easy chaps," Tommy said. "Stuart will resist, but if anyone can achieve this I think it's you two working together. You both have a vested interest in making sure that Stuart doesn't get away with his crime."

Another glance was exchanged between Joseph and Keats, a silent agreement passing between them.

"I will do whatever my captain tells me to do," Keats replied.

"Well then, I say we go and have a word with Stuart," Joseph said. "We know where we shall find him, in the backroom of the tobacco shop."

"We won't be able to come with you," Clara said. "If Stuart sees us hanging around, he may realise this is all a bluff. He needs to believe you worked this out for yourselves. I don't doubt you can do this and that you can impress upon him that it would be in his best interest to come forward and confess to his crime."

Both men were agreed. They all left Joseph's room, and Clara and Tommy watched from a safe distance as Joseph and Keats headed into the tobacco shop.

"I am not usually one for encouraging threats against a suspect," Tommy said to his sister as they huddled against a wall in their thick coats. There was a drizzle of rain in the air, and the snow that had been promised for a handful of days looked like it was about to start falling. "But on this occasion, I think it is exactly what needs to be done. Joseph and Keats are the perfect men for such a task. Stuart won't stand a chance; I don't imagine he did much on the frontline in the war."

"I hope they succeed," Clara said thoughtfully. "I want there to be a good conclusion for Joseph and Keats. When this is over, we're going to make sure that both of them come to the convalescence home."

"Agreed."

Clara pulled her hat firmer over her ears and turned up the collar of her coat. It was the wrong sort of weather to be lurking outside, and she wondered what anybody would think if they saw them there. As long as that person wasn't either Mrs Greaves or her son, she didn't really care.

"Annie has asked that you and John come over for Sunday dinner this weekend," Tommy said softly. "I think she misses you both."

"She misses having me around to nag about my inability to ever carry an umbrella, my habit of ruining all my shoes and my knack for traipsing mud into the house," Clara laughed. "But we would be delighted to come over."

Tommy was pleased; it wasn't quite true that Annie had invited them over, it had been his idea, made on the spur of the moment while they were stood in the cold, but he was sure Annie would not mind. They had both agreed the day before that sooner rather than later they wanted to share their good news with Clara and O'Harris. Tommy felt that over Annie's finest roast dinner was the perfect time to reveal their news, though he would let Annie make the final decision about when she told their family. He was quite content to sit back and let her decide when she deemed it appropriate.

They waited in the rain for almost half an hour. Tommy stopped checking his watch after the first few minutes; it was not helping the time to pass. They were both growing colder and colder and considered diving into one of the nearby shops to warm up, but they decided it was prudent to remain where they were and keep an eye on what was going on.

Joseph and Keats might need backup at some point, both of them were vulnerable individuals and though they had been aroused by their indignation there was no telling what might occur. For that matter, though Tommy had not said it aloud, he had a small concern that one of them would perhaps lose their temper and become violent towards Stuart if he continued to deny his crime. He liked to suppose that both Joseph and Keats had a better grasp on their emotions than that, but the war did funny things to a man. He had seen how angry Keats had become when he realised what Stuart had done and how it had affected Joseph. That sort of fury could easily boil over and erupt.

Tommy wanted to be present just in case the worst occurred, and someone needed to intervene.

"This isn't working," Clara said at last.

"Give them a chance," Tommy responded, though in fairness he had been having his doubts about their odds of success for the last few minutes too.

"Stuart isn't going to cave with just those two hounding him, he has too much to lose," Clara shook her head. "It was too great a leap."

"But we have nothing else. We are short on proof," Tommy shrugged. "If only we had been able to trace the gun used in the crime, that would have been physical proof."

"The evidence we need is in that shop," Clara said firmly, then she marched across the road.

"What are you doing? Clara?"

Tommy darted after his sister. She had already headed around a corner and towards an alleyway that ran behind the buildings and gave access to their yards. Clara was on a mission and didn't stop until she was outside the gate that led into the yard of the tobacco shop. Tommy was agitated at what she was about to do.

"Clara, this is reckless…"

Clara tried the latch on the gate and found that it opened smoothly. There was no lock or bolt to stop her entering the yard. Her momentum did not halt as she crossed to the back door of the building.

Tommy knew they were in trouble now, but he could hardly leave his sister to handle this alone. He followed her as quietly as he could, holding his breath as Clara opened the door and stepped into a small stockroom. The smell of tobacco was overwhelming in the tiny space with its narrow window, and he had to stifle a cough.

Clara kept moving, heading next through a doorway into a narrow back room that served as a sitting room and kitchen. They could hear Keats and Joseph at the front of the shop, arguing with Stuart, his mother occasionally making interjections. Clara paused just a moment to listen, then carried on with her errand.

Tommy no longer dared to ask her what she was doing or try to stop her, for fear of making too much noise. He had a hunch what she was about, and though her methods were questionable he agreed with her idea.

Clara took a quick look around the sitting room, before heading toward a staircase that ran up the far side. Tommy could only follow as they silently climbed upstairs to the bedrooms of the house. The first door immediately off the stairs proved to be Mrs Greaves' bedroom and they ignored it, travelling instead to the second room which proved to be Stuart's.

No words were exchanged as they began to search the room. Tommy knew what Clara was looking for, he just hoped they could find it. He went to a chest of drawers just like the one he used to keep his own old service revolver in. Tucking it among his socks had seemed a strangely fitting place for a gun that had brought so much misery to him during the war yet had somehow been impossible to part with afterwards.

It turned out, Stuart thought the same way. The revolver was sitting on top of a pair of grey socks. Tommy picked it out and showed it to Clara.

"Good," she said, without ceasing her own searching.

"Isn't this what you wanted to find?"

"It was one of the things I wanted to find," Clara corrected. "There is one other piece of evidence in this case – the envelope Stuart used to deliver the money to Keats. If we can find a match for it here, then we really have something."

Tommy could see she was intent on searching the room top to bottom for just such an envelope and nothing he said would deter her. However, despite a thorough hunt through every conceivable place an envelope might be kept they found none. Meanwhile, downstairs, the argument was getting heated and Clara heard Mrs Greaves shouting that she was going to summon the police.

Time was running out.

"Not here," Clara concluded angrily. "But then Stuart does not appear to be much of a correspondent. There are no writing materials here at all. So let us suppose he took the envelope from his mother." Tommy cringed as Clara dashed into the room next door and began another urgent search. He stood in the doorway, listening to the discord downstairs and fearing being discovered.

"Clara!" He hissed, deciding he could bear it no more and they needed to leave.

At that moment Clara stood up with an envelope clasped in her hand.

"A light cream envelope with a distinctive impressed mark on the flap. Look familiar?"

From her pocket Clara produced the rumpled envelope Keats had given them.

"You have been carrying that around all this time?" Tommy asked in surprise.

"Of course, in case we found its double, which we just did."

"We better hurry, because things are going badly downstairs, and I think Mrs Greaves is going to summon the police."

"Good," Clara said with a sinister smile. "Then we have one last thing to do. We need to jog our only witness' memory and finally resolve this case. I have a job for you Tommy."

"Oh dear," Tommy groaned.

Chapter Twenty-Eight

Nothing was working. Stuart was denying everything and placing Joseph and Keats in a worse position than before. Now his mother had threatened to call the police, yet retreat did not seem an option.

Keats was furious, his fists clenched and a real danger emerging that he might decide to simply beat the truth out of Stuart. Joseph was just about holding his friend in check, but his own temper was perilously close to exploding.

The man before him had cost him three months of his life. He had endured the hardships of prison because of this man who just stared smugly at him and denied ever doing anything wrong. It was almost too much to bear.

Keats was about to lose control, and Joseph knew there would be nothing he could do to hold him back – or, rather, there was nothing he cared to do – when the shop door burst open.

The sudden jangle of the bell grabbed all of their attentions, Joseph and Keats spinning around to see not the policeman they had irrationally expected, but an ordinary looking man with a hat pulled down over his eyes and a scarf around his mouth. He stepped into the shop and lifted a revolver which he pointed at Mrs Greaves.

"I want all the money from your safe!"

For a moment, Joseph thought he had stumbled into a dream, seeing a repeat of the robbery his friend was supposed to have committed. Keats gave a muffled cry of alarm, while behind the counter Mrs Greaves gave a wail.

"He is back!"

"Mother!"

Stuart went to grab her as she seemed fit to fall down, which was when Tommy whipped off the scarf and revealed himself.

"Pretty convincing," he said with a smile.

Clara appeared in the shop doorway and hurried to Mrs Greaves.

"He looks just like the man who robbed me," Mrs Greaves said, trembling as Clara approached.

There was a tall stool behind the counter which Clara retrieved for her and had her sit upon.

"He looks just the same? Even the gun?" Clara asked.

"Mother..."

Clara cast a scowl at Stuart that sent him into silence. The look in her eyes told him she knew what he had done, and she could prove it. He took a step away from his mother, his gaze now flitting around the room as he considered how he might escape.

"Yes, that is just the gun the robber used. Now I see it, the memory comes back clearly. The gun could be identical," Mrs Greaves was wide-eyed as she stared at Tommy.

Clara waved her brother forward and he placed the gun on the shop counter.

"There is a good reason why this gun looks identical," he said to

Mrs Greaves. "This is your son's service revolver. The one he used to threaten you when he robbed the shop that day. It is not loaded. You can examine it if you want."

"Where did you get that!" Stuart snapped. "You have been in my room...!"

He hesitated as he realised he had just admitted that the gun was his. Had he remained silent, he could have pretended the gun had nothing to do with him and who could prove otherwise?

His mother glanced up in his direction.

"You have kept a gun in my home all these years?"

"It was a souvenir from the war," Stuart gabbled, there being no point pretending it was not his now. "All the lads kept theirs. I have no bullets for it."

Mrs Greaves stared at the gun.

"You pointed this at me." "No, Mother, they are making you think things that aren't true!"

Clara carefully placed the fresh envelope she had found in Mrs Greaves' room before the woman.

"This is the stationary you like to use?"

"Yes," Mrs Greaves said numbly.

"You have searched our home!" Stuart barked, though his indignation was not helping.

"This is the envelope that contained some of the proceeds from the robbery of your shop. It was given anonymously to Keats in an effort to frame him for the crime."

Clara placed the second envelope in front of the shopkeeper. The woman gave a thin gasp, now glad of the stool to sit upon as shock overcame her.

"It was you, Stuart!"

"No, Mother! They are lying!"

"We know why you did it," Tommy interjected before Stuart could say anything more. "You wanted to buy an engagement ring for your lady friend at the *Ruddy Mallard*. We have evidence you spent the remainder of the stolen money on a ring just after the robbery."

Stuart fell silent, there was nothing much he could say to that. His mother now had her gaze fixed on him.

"Lady friend? What is this, Stuart?"

"I was going to tell you," Stuart winced. "The time was never right."

"I suspect you had no intention of telling your mother anything," Clara rebuked him. "You believe your mother is dying, which is why you needed to find yourself another woman to live off. You would have married only after your mother had died and could not object to your mercenary behaviour."

Mrs Greaves shuddered at the statement.

"You know I am ill?"

"Of course I know," Stuart snapped at her. "You are not exactly good at keeping secrets. I saw the medicine bottle in your shopping basket."

"And, you said nothing?" Mrs Greaves blinked. "You just went behind my back and started to plan out how you would live without me?"

Mrs Greaves was quivering with fury, she almost seemed to vibrate before Clara. Abruptly, she rose from the stool and stormed towards her son before he could react she slapped him hard across his face.

"You threatened me with a gun! You stole the money I had worked hard for! All so you could marry someone who would replace me when I was gone! What sort of son have I raised!"

Stuart clutched his face, unable to respond.

"I think about now is the time to take Stuart to the police station and present them with our evidence," Clara suggested. "Even if he does not care to confess, we have proof enough to implicate him as the real robber of this shop."

"You will confess to the police!" Mrs Greaves confronted her son. "You shall clear Joseph's name, and you will do one thing in your life that is not selfish!""Mother?" Stuart stared at his mother, aghast.

"Do you hear me?"

"Yes, Mother."

"You will confess your crime to the police, do you understand?"

"Yes," Stuart said weakly.

Tommy glanced at Keats and Joseph.

"Think its time for you two to step in," he nodded at them.

Keats needed no further prodding. He moved forward and took Stuart's arm. Joseph joined him and took the other. Between them they marched Stuart to the shop door. He hung almost limp in their grasp, his gaze returning to his mother, hoping for some sign of forgiveness and respite from his doom.

Just as they were about to leave Mrs Greaves spoke up.

"Mr Nunn, Mr Keats, please, once you have dealt with my son, would you return here? We have a lot to talk about and I owe you an apology Mr Nunn."

Joseph quietly nodded at her, then he continued out the shop with Stuart an unprotesting prisoner between him and Keats.

Mrs Greaves watched them leave, the horror of what was occurring dawning on her. Clara was concerned for her health and persuaded the woman to follow her into the back sitting room, while Tommy turned the sign on the shop door and put the bolt across to give them some peace and quiet. Mrs Greaves semi-collapsed on the sofa almost as soon as she entered the back room, her hand clasped over her heart. Clara grew worried when she seemed to be having trouble breathing, her breaths coming in great, heavy gulps. She sat down beside Mrs

Greaves' and clasped her hand.

"Maybe I should summon a doctor?" She suggested, thinking that Dr Cunningham would surely come at once if he were called.

Mrs Greaves shook her head.

"It is just the shock of it all. My own son robbed me! What sort of monster have I nurtured in this home all these years?"

Clara knew of nothing she could say to ease the woman's distress, instead she promised to sit with her a while.

"Let me make you a cup of tea," Clara suggested.

Mrs Greave nodded meekly. Tommy took a seat opposite her while Clara went about the task of finding the kettle and filling it with water.

"I am sorry about the shock I gave you marching in with a gun like that," he said. "I just hoped to jog your memory."

"You certainly did that," Mrs Greaves said bitterly. "But I am not angry at you. I am not even angry at Stuart. I am angry at myself. I must have failed my son somehow to turn him into such a creature. Somewhere along the line, he lost his way, and I never saw it."

"I don't think it is as simple as that," Tommy consoled her.

Mrs Greaves was having none of it. Though they remained with her for an hour, they could not convince her that she was not responsible for her son's actions. By the time they were satisfied she was not in any danger of collapse, and were ready to go home, they had done nothing to change her mind, and it was apparent no words they said ever could.

Mrs Greaves believed that somehow her son's failings were all her fault rather than his – and perhaps that explained more about Stuart's personality and his actions than anything else they had heard or seen.

The following Sunday, they all sat around the dining room table in the Fitzgerald's home. Annie had decided to cook lamb for a change, a meat she didn't usually buy as it could be quite expensive, especially at this time of year. But she had decided that this was a special occasion and deserved something different.

Not only had Clara resolved her latest case, but she had received a letter stating that no further action would be taken regarding the defamation case brought against her by Mr Maguire.

After Gilbert had his friend cast his eye over the papers, they had been told there was enough to get the police involved and they had handed all the evidence of corruption and fraud to Inspector Park-Coombs. Not long afterwards, Mr Maguire had been taken in for questioning. The evidence was pretty damning and was made worse when the police obtained a statement from Mr Florentine, the planning officer who had been bribed. Mr Maguire attempted to assuage his involvement in the matter, swearing he was as much an innocent dupe as the people he had been selling bungalows to, but he was not convincing anyone.

Maguire asked for his solicitor shortly after he learned that Florentine was telling the police everything and squarely dropping him in trouble. When the solicitor arrived and heard what was going on, he realised that Maguire was in serious trouble.

Inspector Park-Coombs took the opportunity to take the man aside and persuade him that the defamation case against Clara and Tommy should be dropped sooner rather than later, under the circumstances. He was quite insistent on the subject, though the solicitor could not fathom why it mattered so much to him.

In any case, there were far graver matters to worry about than a defamation case that was most likely going to be thrown out of court. After a quick discussion with his client, the solicitor was happy to type up a hasty letter which explained that the matter had been dropped and handed it to Park-Coombs.

The inspector delivered it to Clara in person, a smile upon his usually serious face when he presented it to her on the doorstep. He offered no explanation of the contents of the letter, leaving Clara to discover that after he had wished her farewell and headed for home.

Clara had almost shed a tear when she read the letter. It had not occurred to her how worried she had been about the defamation case and the unwanted publicity. The relief she felt took her by surprise and she had to ask O'Harris to read the letter as she could not quite believe her eyes.

"It does say what I think it says?" She asked him, a tad anxious she was misunderstanding the missive.

"It does," O'Harris grinned. "The defamation case has been dropped."

Clara laughed and clapped her hands in delight.

"Oh, I am so glad to no longer have that to worry about!"

Mr Maguire, on the other hand, had a lot to worry about.

He was facing serious charges of fraud and bribery. Mullins dead was no use to him; he found attempting to place the blame on the deceased man only earned him an amused look from the inspector. The police had enough evidence to warrant them taking a closer look at Maguire's business arrangements and it was not long before they found further documentation of his dubious activities. Maguire's cunning had only gone so far. He had failed to cover his tracks sufficiently, and there was paperwork in his offices and home that would lead to his downfall. He had kept certain letters as insurance in case Mullins ever considered turning on him, now those same letters would become the metaphorical noose around his neck.

There was still no news concerning what would happen to the

bungalows, though since they were built on the back of bribes and corruption there was a fair chance they would be knocked down and the land restored to common grazing land.

Though Annie had not had the opportunity to speak to Miss Carter on the subject, she was certain the woman would be delighted to know what had occurred and would be satisfied that they had done all they could. Mr Maguire was finally getting the justice he deserved.

Stuart Greaves was also facing prison time. Not only had he perverted the course of justice by trying to shift the blame for his own crimes onto Keats, but he had robbed his mother in the first place. Mrs Greaves did not want to press charges against her son, but in a criminal matter such as robbery, it did not matter what she wanted. The inspector was also stinging from arresting the wrong man in the first place. Greaves was not going to have an easy time of things.

There had been no comment from the landlady of the *Ruddy Mallard* concerning the arrest of her fiancé. Keats had gone back to the pub the evening after Stuart had been arrested, not sure what he would say to the women, but knowing he had to say something. He had wondered what reception he would get, but the landlady was very willing to see him.

It had not taken long for news of Stuart's arrest to reach her. When Keats entered the pub, she immediately waved him over to the bar. He was ready for an argument and recriminations, instead the landlady instantly poured him a pint and insisted he sit on a stool by the bar instead of his usual corner. Keats noticed she had already taken off the engagement ring.

Before he could say anything, she declared she would make him a sandwich and he was not to move.

She said nothing about Stuart, focusing instead on fussing around Keats just like his mother would. It seemed she felt used as well.

Mrs Greaves was also doing her best to make amends. She had asked both men to work at the tobacco shop, reinstating Joseph in his former position and employing Keats to make deliveries.

She would need all the help she could get, as she had decided to have the operation Dr Cunningham had recommended.

They learned all this from O'Harris, who had paid a visit to Keats after he failed to show up at the home on that first day he was invited. O'Harris could not help but wonder if the landlady had been involved in the robbery, at least after the fact when Stuart was trying to shift blame away from himself. If she had been involved, Stuart did not mention her. They would never know if it had been the landlady who had plotted to frame Keats, or whether Stuart had miraculously thought the scheme up all by himself.

Tommy had spent the day after Stuart's arrest writing a letter to the relevant authorities concerning Joseph's Victoria Cross. The case would not be closed until he had ensured Joseph's name was reinstated on the list of all those who had been awarded the honour. In his letter, he made it plain that Joseph was still acting in a brave and self-sacrificing manner even in civilian life, being prepared to sacrifice himself for another who he felt would not survive prison, and for whom he felt responsible.

Tommy would be the first to admit that he had laid on the praise rather thick in the letter, but he felt the situation justified such prose. With any luck it would not be long before they had the news that Joseph's VC award was being reinstated.

O'Harris, meanwhile, had made sure that Joseph and Keats finally came to the convalescence home. Neither man had been terribly keen; both had seemed to think that they were failures for not being able to deal with their problems on their own. Fortunately, O'Harris was remarkably persuasive, and it helped that Clara had said she would forgo her usual fee for solving the case on the proviso that both Joseph and Keats went to the Home and participated in the various treatment programmes. The two men couldn't really argue with that.

It was early days, but O'Harris was hopeful that the men would be able to resurrect their old lives with the assistance of his team.

Sitting around the dining table that Sunday, the mouth-watering smell of lamb roasting wafting from the kitchen, Clara felt she had every right to be satisfied with the outcome of both cases. Maguire was finally unmasked as a con-artist and the real culprit for the tobacco shop robbery was going to face justice. Not to mention Joseph and Keats were at last going to receive treatment for their mental war wounds.

Tommy appeared with the roasted lamb carved and sitting on a serving plate. It was unusual for Annie to allow anyone other than herself to bring the food through to the table, but Clara did not give it much thought. Annie was just behind her husband with a dish of potatoes and a jug of homemade mint sauce. Tommy quickly took the items off her, as if they were too heavy for his wife to handle.

O'Harris gave Clara a nudge, but she had not noticed. O'Harris now watched Tommy intently, as he fussed around Annie, removing from her hands every bowl or plate she dared to bring through from the kitchen, even the gravy boat. Tommy was in danger of earning Annie's wrath at his antics, her face becoming a picture of discord. O'Harris decided it would be prudent to intervene.

"Something you want to tell us, old man?"

Tommy glanced at his friend and realised O'Harris had seen through him. A strange smile came onto his face, he looked suddenly coy and turned to Annie.

"I think they are on to us."

Clara glanced up.

"On to what?"

O'Harris laughed.

"Hurry up and give us your news before the great detective manages to catch up!"

"Are you sure?" Annie asked her husband.

"I can't wait any longer," Tommy declared.

Clara was frowning, still oblivious to what further news they could have.

"We are celebrating," Tommy continued. "That is why it is roast lamb and not beef as usual."

"Solving two cases in a week is certainly something to celebrate," Clara agreed. "Especially when one of those cases was solved by our very own Annie, who showed great resilience and determination, not to mention initiative, going out there and finding out what Maguire had truly been up to him."

Annie shook her head at Clara.

"I'm not celebrating that," she informed them. "I am not the sort of person to blow my own trumpet. That is not what this is about."

"Well, now I am intrigued," Clara said.

Beside her, O'Harris' grin was only growing, partly because he was hugely amused Clara had not realised what was going on.

"You better get on with it, Annie," Tommy hissed in a stage whisper to his wife. "There are too many detectives around this table, they will guess if we don't hurry up."

Annie caught Clara's gaze and held it. The smile that came onto her face couldn't have been bigger or more genuine.

"I am going to have a baby, Clara,"

"A baby?" Clara just stared at her, a little overcome by the news.

"Congratulations, old man," O'Harris put his hand across the table so he could shake with Tommy.

Clara had been stunned into silence.

"Say something Clara," Annie said to her friend. "It's not like you to become tongue-tied."

"I am just... I am just so happy for you Annie," Clara said smiling broadly. "I am so, so happy for you."

"You know, with all this new baby stuff we will have to be buying, we will be needing a little bit extra financially," Tommy said grinning at his sister. "So I was thinking of asking my employer for a pay raise?"

"We are partners, therefore we split everything equally," Clara smirked at him. "But I'm sure it wouldn't hurt to take on a few extra cases just to help out. The next few months are certainly going to be a busy time."

"Make the most of it, old man, won't be long and you'll have not only a new mouth to feed but someone else to boss you around once they get old enough to do so," O'Harris jested to Tommy.

"I couldn't be happier about that, I can't wait," Tommy grinned back. "With any luck we'll have a girl and she'll be just like her mother, then there will be no hope for me at all."

Annie poked him hard with her elbow in the ribs.

Tommy expelled a puff of air dramatically as if she had hurt him.

"See?"

They all began to laugh and chuckle, as they settled down to their celebratory meal. It had proved to be a very good week and the future for them all was looking very bright. By next Christmas there would be fourth at their table and the Fitzgerald family would be growing once again.

"You know," O'Harris said with a smirk, "I think I should celebrate the fact that I realised what your news was ahead of my famous detective wife."

"I had an inkling!" Clara lied.

"Oh, hark at you!" Annie scoffed. "You were oblivious."

Clara glanced back at the lamb, mildly embarrassed that she had, indeed, been oblivious.

"Stick to solving murder, old thing," Tommy consoled her. "You're good at that."

Clara gave him a scowl, which set him off laughing, before long they were all engulfed by the merriment.

"Of course, I knew, I just did not want to spoil the moment," Clara insisted.

"Of course," O'Harris chuckled at her. "We all believe you!"

Clara pulled a face at him, which only set them to laughing once again.

Enjoyed this Book?

You can make a difference

As an independent writer reviews of my books are hugely important to help my work reach a wider audience. If you haven't already, I would love it if you could take five minutes to review this book on .
the platform you purchased it from.
Thank you very much!

The Clara Fitzgerald Series

Have you read them all?

Memories of the Dead
The first mystery
Flight of Fancy
The second mystery
Murder in Mink
The third mystery
Carnival of Criminals
The fourth mystery
Mistletoe and Murder
The fifth mystery
The Poison Pen
The sixth mystery
Grave Suspicions of Murder
The seventh mystery

The Woman Died Thrice
The eighth mystery
Murder and Mascara
The ninth mystery
The Green Jade Dragon
The tenth mystery
The Monster at the Window
The eleventh mystery
Murder on the Mary Jane
The twelfth mystery
The Missing Wife
The thirteenth mystery
The Traitor's Bones
The fourteenth mystery
The Fossil Murder
The fifteenth mystery
Mr Lynch's Prophecy
The sixteenth mystery
Death at the Pantomime
The seventeenth mystery
The Cowboy's Crime
The eighteenth mystery
The Trouble with Tortoises
The nineteenth mystery
The Valentine Murder
The twentieth mystery
A Body Out of Time
The twenty-first mystery
The Dog Show Affair
The twenty-second mystery

The Unlucky Wedding Guest
The twenty-third mystery
Worse Things Happen at Sea
The twenty-fourth mystery
A Diet of Death
The twenty-fifth mystery
Brilliant Chang Returns
The twenty-sixth mystery
Storm in a Teacup
The twenty-seventh mystery
The Dog Theft Mystery
The twenty-eighth mystery
The Day the Zeppelin Came
The twenty-ninth mystery
The Mystery of Mallory
The thirtieth mystery
Death at the Sun Club
The thirty-first mystery
The Disappearance of Emily Potter
The thirty-second mystery
Bright Young Dead Things
The thirty-third mystery
The Price of Honour
The thirty-fourth mystery

A New Series from Evelyn James

The Gentlemen Detective Mysteries

The Gentleman Detective

Norwich 1898.

Colonel Bainbridge is wondering if it is time to hang up his magnifying glass when a pugilist dies unexpectedly, and an innocent man is accused of his murder.

Distracted by trying to save a friend from the noose, Bainbridge finds himself investigating the murky world of street fighting and match fixing.

Can he determine who really killed the boxer Simon One-Foot or will a innocent man end up swinging for a crime he could not have committed?

The Gentleman Detective is the first novel in a brand new series from the creator of the Clara Fitzgerald Mysteries, Evelyn James.

Start your investigation with Colonel Bainbridge today!

Available on Amazon

About the Author

Evelyn James (aka Sophie Jackson) began her writing career in 2003 working in traditional publishing before embracing the world of ebooks and self-publishing. She has written over 80 books, available on a variety of platforms, both fiction and non-fiction.

You can find out more about Sophie's various titles at her website
www.sophie-jackson.com
or connect through social media on Facebook
www.facebook.com/SophieJacksonAuthor
and if you fancy sending an email do so at
sophiejackson.author@gmail.com

Copyright © 2024 by Evelyn James

No form of generative AI was used in the creation of this work

All rights reserved.

The moral right of Evelyn James to be identified as the author of this work has been asserted by her in accordance with the Copyright, Designs and Patents Act 1988.

All the characters in this book are fictitious, and any resemblance to actual persons living or dead is purely coincidental.

No part of this publication may be reproduced, stored in a retrieval system or transmitted in any form or by any means, without the prior permission in writing of the publisher, nor to be otherwise circulated in any form of binding or cover other than that in which it is published without a similar condition, including this condition, being imposed on the subsequent purchaser.

Evelyn James is a pen name for Sophie Jackson.

To contact about licensing or permission rights email sophiejackson.author@gmail.com

Printed in Dunstable, United Kingdom